A GLIMPSE OF TIGER

HERMAN RAUCHER

DIVERSIONBOOKS

Also by Herman Raucher
Maynard's House
Summer of '42
There Should Have Been Castles

Diversion Books
A Division of Diversion Publishing Corp.
443 Park Avenue South, Suite 1008
New York, New York 10016
www.DiversionBooks.com

For more information, email info@diversionbooks.com
For more from Herman Raucher, visit www.hermanraucher.com

First Diversion Books edition May 2015.
Print ISBN: 978-1-62681-892-7
eBook ISBN: 978-1-62681-808-8

For M. K., who is always there

1

Subway people, whatever their individual identities, share three things in common: They are semihuman; they are going somewhere; and they do not speak to one another. They merely carry their isolation from one place to the next, and at the end of some mystical time period, they simply reverse the process. There are, however, a few of the species that subway folks themselves do not take to. They do not take to people who have fits, or throw up, or release their bladders, or die, or beg. The last of the aforementioned are the most burdensome in that they can cost money. Watching people die or wet or get sick—that's *free*. It can also be stepped over or around. But beggars—beggars are a no-no. Especially blind beggars. With guitars. And helpers.

And so, when the door at the rear end of the next to last car of the Sea Beach Express slid open, and when the tall and fairly decently dressed blind man with dark glasses groped his way in, the passengers pressed back as one and made room for him, fearing perhaps that blindness was contagious.

Behind the blind man came his helper, a pretty girl, slight, in unisex attire, her hair tucked in under her Jackie Coogan cap, her slender, almost fragile figure snugly encased in the bell-bottom trousers of the day. She closed the door, not without effort, then helped steady the tall young man who stood with spread legs until feeling her touch. The young man then rattled the coins in his tin cup—attention, please! Then he strummed his guitar and began to sing, carefully picking his way through the subway car in the manner of a faltering leper.

His style of singing and playing was barely professional. And yet there was something terribly touching about the blind man singing of his plight, in a voice that carried little anguish and less emotion. As a result, the girl in his wake captured the clink of many a coin.

> Don't see nothin' but trouble,
> Trouble on the dark road ahead;
> Keep stubbin' my toe on the sunshine,
> Thinkin' that maybe I'm dead.
>
> Don't see nothin' but sorrow,
> Sorrow on the rim of the night,
> Lord, you sure threw me a curve ball,
> When you went and turned off my light.

The blind man continued strumming his guitar, but it was the young girl who sang the song's release, utilizing a small and tremulous balladlike folk voice, more nearly that of a choirboy.

Does anyone know where he's going?

Does anyone here really care?
If he walked himself out on the highway...
Would the big Mack truck be there?

The blind man and the girl then sang the last chorus together, a plaintive summing up of his loneliness and fear.

Big Mack truck,
Big Mack truck,
Bearin' down on me...
Big Mack truck on the highway,
Oh, say, can you see, can you seeeeeeeee...
Oh, say, can you see—
Can you see?

By the last chorus the passengers were so filled with guilt at having the power of sight that they kicked in generously. The girl then led the blind man into the next car, and the next, and the next. They averaged $1.75 a subway car that morning and did six such cars before taking a urine break.

The subway men's room, like most of the genre, was not a place where one would normally hold a garden party. It was dull, dirty and graffiti. The men who frequented it were either habitués or passersby who couldn't hold out. And they all, regardless of where they came from or what their life-style was, stood up against the wall like horses in a starting gate.

Down at the end of the starting line, beyond the last urinal, the blind man stood before the grimy mirror, trying to run a comb through his tangle of coal-black hair. Three times did the comb disappear before any semblance of order took place on his thatchwork. But what was patently obvious from his actions was that the young man was not blind at all. Not the least bit. And to point that up further, he removed his dark glasses and a pair of large brown eyes went beaming at his own reflection.

The girl stood adjacent, holding the guitar as though it were a bass fiddle, while examining the coins in the cup. A few of the urinating men did double takes at the girl but wouldn't have known what to do or say if indeed there were a girl under all that boyish clothing. So they merely went on doing their duty and then got the hell out.

The girl came up with the total. "Ten dollars and fifty cents. Three Canadian dimes. Two slugs. A cuff link. And a Humphrey button."

The tall young man turned, smiled, took the guitar from her, slipped the strap over his head, and then started out of the men's room. As he passed the men who stood against the wall, he gently prodded each one in turn. "Keep up the good work...You're doing fine...Attaboy...You bet."

The men looked over their shoulders at the exiting madman only to be confronted by the girl, who held the tin cup up to them while demurely lowering her eyes. None of the men contributed, mostly because it would have been inconvenient for them to drop what they were doing.

The girl followed the tall man out of the men's room as he played and sang the old favorite, "By a waterfall, I'm calling you-oo-oo-oo..."

2

The two figures in the back seat of the taxicab were barely discernible within the moving vehicle, at first appearing only as demonic shadows being drawn through the night lights of New York. Only later did they appear as people. As a result there was a gathering air of the *misterioso* to their hushed conversation.

Up front the interested cabby drove, his head cocked over his right shoulder—thoroughly tuned in on the dialogue behind him.

The dark-visaged young man in the dinner jacket was speaking, and he was more than a trifle upset. "Annabelle, I swear, this is senseless. It proves nothing. If you have the baby, your husband is bound to find out. He's not a *complete* fool. And in his position with the government—I mean, *really*, Annabelle, the man *is* a Congressman."

The pretty girl with the long straight hair was distraught. She ran her hands over and over across her chic evening dress. "I know, I know! But what can we do? We have to do *something!*"

"Get rid of it."

The cabby almost plowed into the car ahead, which would have been unfortunate since it was a police car.

"Roland, no! I can't do that! I've *told* you!"

The man was displeased and hurled himself into a deep sulk. "You carry Catholicism too far."

"I'm not Catholic."

"You carry your *Lutheranism* too far."

"I'm not Lutheran."

He barked at her. "Then what the hell *are* you?"

"I'm pregnant!" And she turned all soft and sobby. "And don't snap at me. It's not *my* fault. God—*men!*"

The man made an attempt to assuage her. "Annabelle, please. Maintain your poise."

But she was very upset, and her voice rose two octaves. "Roland, I am seven months pregnant! Seven months! And you tell me to maintain my *poise*—"

The man pondered her last remark. "Hmmmmmmm. Seven months, you say. Are you certain?"

"Certainly I'm certain."

"Hmmmmmmmmm. That's peculiar. *I* only know you *three* months."

"Oh, don't you try to wiggle out of it on a technicality." And she turned haughtily away from him, choosing instead to look out her window at the speeding streetscape.

In a few moments he spoke again, and the girl coiled up because she knew what was coming. "Annabelle, excuse me. I don't want to appear rude, but…the responsibility, it seems, isn't mine."

"That will be up to a jury to decide, won't it?"

The man lit a cigarette, inhaled and exhaled with great self-assurance. "Have to be a pretty corrupt, graft-ridden, and cockamamie jury to hang *me* with the rap. Especially if I can prove that I was out of town or in jail...or both."

She spun on him. "You're all alike, all of you. You're always so innocent. I don't know how I get to bed down with *any* of you—you're never *around!* Well, Roland, I did not come about this conception immaculately, let me tell you."

The cabby was taking it all in while risking all three of their lives in traffic. But it was worth it. He'd have another great anecdote for his book, *I Hack New York.*

The man in the back remained pensive for a few more minutes, during which time the cabby ran two red lights and narrowly missed a half dozen gesticulating pedestrians. "Annabelle, listen," he said, "I know what we can do."

"What?"

"It's drastic, but...I mean, if *your* husband or *my* parole officer ever found out, there'd be the devil to pay, wouldn't there?"

"Roland, what? For God's sake, what?"

"Well"—he was dramatically controlled as he outlined his plan—"we'll need some help from the Japanese, of course, but with what we have on them, plus a little pressure from the State Department in Malaysia—" He glanced out the window. "Oh. We're here."

They were indeed there, in front of the Sherry-Netherland Hotel, and the cabby sat pop-eyed at the wheel of his idling car, hanging in the middle of the unfinished tale.

The tall man leaned forward and handed the cabby a bill, relying on a soft voice fraught with inner meanings. "You have children?"

"Huh?" said the cabby.

"You never saw me." It wasn't even a veiled threat. It was a blatant promise of death. The cabby sat there, immobile, choosing to not look at his two disembarking passengers, not realizing until later that what he had in his hand was not a five-dollar bill, nor even a one. It was a card from a Monopoly game and it read "You Are Assessed for Street Repairs."

The tall man and the angular girl had, by then, walked arm in arm into the hotel, sweeping in like the royal family. Others, similarly dressed, were also moving through the lobby in opulent pairings, looking three times worthy of the plush carpeting that their feet never seemed to touch. Casually they all consulted the announcement board, which, in white letters on maroon velvet, declared: UJA BANQUET. THE CRYSTAL ROOM.

The elevator was every bit as elegant as its passengers, all of whom took the ascension in hallowed silence. That is, except for the tall dark man and the pretty girl on his arm. They had another small dialogue going, new words in the air to buffet and titillate the bystanders in the vicinity.

"That's what he told me," the man said in a pseudo whisper that hit everyone's ears like a trumpet fanfare, not because it was loud, but because their radarscopes were wide open. "And he ought to know. He's been with the *New York Times* for over ten years."

The girl evidenced interest and surprise. "And he said that this entire hotel was alive with call girls? *This* hotel?"

"Not the *entire* hotel, Rhoda. Just one floor. And all you have to do is knock on any door. *Any* door."

"Which floor?" asked the girl.

And all the passengers stood there at eighteen-degree angles, Towers of Pisa leaning toward the tall man. The men, especially. But the elevator came to a climactic halt, and the door opened, and, as if on cue, all the male passengers immediately hated the elevator operator, who doltishly broke the silence with "Crystal Room. United Jewish Appeal, please."

The tall man and the pretty girl, known to a select few as Luther and Tiger, swept out of the elevator, leaving the other shoe never to drop. The other passengers followed dumbly.

The Crystal Room was appropriately large and predictably lavish. The music that played was either the "Lester Lanin Fox Trot" or the "Meyer Davis Waltz." And a few of the guests were already on the dance floor, recapturing their youth while refracturing the same vertebrae they had mutilated a year earlier at a similar fund raising.

But most of the crowd was seated at the many large round tables, in the middle of which were cardboard placards that proclaimed in huge Arabic (Arabic!) numbers, each table's numerical designation. Also, at each place setting there was a name card. And each guest whose name appeared on a card had paid, in advance, $250 for the right to wrestle with a corpulent Maryland pheasant.

Luther and Tiger hung pretty much around the checkroom until it seemed as though all who were coming had already arrived. After that they sauntered laughingly into the Crystal Room and casually surveyed the terrain. There were a few empty places, for it was not uncommon at such functions for people to pay the $250 tariff and then not show up. And so it was reasonable to assume that the chairs that were unoccupied by 9:30 P.M. would remain unoccupied for the entire evening. None of this thoughtful strategy was new to Luther. Also, if there was something he loved more than a Maryland pheasant, it had not yet flown to New York.

The diners had just about consumed their fruit salad and were well into their soup when Luther scanned the room in search of a table that had two adjacent unoccupied chairs. There were three such tables. Luther turned to Tiger and assumed the guise of a French maître d'. "Your *sélection*, madame. You may 'ave Table Numbair Three, a good group, very *bon*. Or if you like, Numbair Nine, very close to ze dance floor if you are so inclined. Or there is Numbair Twenty-three, a bit to ze rear but very close to ze exit, which is not a bad idea either, eh?"

Tiger squinted through her imaginary lorgnette and grandly selected. "Number Nine, please, Henri. It was my number on the Sorbonne Field Hockey Team."

"But of course," said Luther, and he took her by the arm, and they ambled gaily across to Table No. Nine, which, like the other tables mentioned, had two empty side-by-side seats.

The guests looked up at them, and Luther and Tiger smiled in return. Luther then picked up and carefully examined the names on the place cards. And then, so that all could see and hear, he smiled nicely at Tiger and said, "Here we are, dear." He then addressed the guests at the table with disarming charm. "Good evening. Mr. and Mrs. Jack Bergman couldn't make it tonight. I'm their nephew, Seymour Fleischman, from St. Louis. And this is my wife, Shelda." Tiger did a sweet curtsy, and the men at the table began to rise politely. "No, no." Luther intervened with a raised hand. "Please. It's our own fault for being so late.

Please, go back to your soup."

The men hovered in midair like Jewish hummingbirds, then descended gently back onto their chairs. Luther than held the chair for Tiger, and she smiled graciously, sitting down with consummate grace. Luther did likewise, and smiling at the fruit salad and then at Tiger, he lifted his spoon and said to her, "Spoons up?"

And she raised her spoon and said, "Spoons up," and they plunged into their fruit salad, for the night was sumptuous and they had some catching up to do.

And, oh, it was a fine meal, the best they had had in some time. Not even the society repast they had crashed out at East Hampton could compare with it, proving the efficacy of Luther's observation that "when you're hungry, the whole world is Jewish."

Somewhere around the baked Alaska, the fifty-five-year-old man next to Luther seemed deeply troubled. His name was Mossberg, and since the salad, he had been debating with himself whether or not to address Luther. Finally, looking and sounding like Sam Levene, he tapped Luther's arm politely and said, "Excuse me, Mr. Fleischman."

It took Luther a scant moment to realize that that was *him.* Then he turned and smiled. "Yes?"

"I know your uncle from way back. I'm an old friend. Therefore, may I ask, whatever became of him this evening?"

"Gallbladder," said Luther, and he tried silently to relate to Mossberg that it was too painful a subject and that he'd prefer not to discuss it.

But Mossberg was so taken aback that he didn't pick up on Luther's reluctance. "Gallbladder! Since when?"

"Oh, I'd say—since four o'clock this afternoon." And

Tiger reached over and touched Luther's hand gently because she knew how difficult it was for Luther even to think about, let alone discuss.

Mossberg, in mini-shock, became sagely reflective. "You just never know, do you? A healthy man like Jack Bergman." And he turned to his wife and said, "Jack Bergman had a four o'clock gallbladder attack."

Mrs. Mossberg, a nice lady with a mouthful of dessert, was quite concerned with the medical bulletin. "Oh, tsk-tsk-tsk," she said, nodding her head on each "tsk" so that it seemed as though her neck, not her mouth, were making the clucking noise.

Mossberg turned again to Luther, hurt and disbelief on his face. "He didn't mention my name to you?"

"Well, he *was* in great pain."

Mossberg was persistent in his concern, a Semitic trait that had no doubt brought about the capture and undoing of Eichmann. "But we planned on sitting next to each other. I can't *believe* he said *nothing*."

Luther tried very hard to remember. He was successful. "He *did* mumble a name. I thought it was his doctor. What did you say your name was?"

"Mossberg. Mossberg Hats."

"Hmmmm," said Luther and he turned to Tiger. "Did Uncle Jack ever mention that we'd be sitting next to Mossberg Hats?"

Tiger deliberated. "Mossberg Hats. Hmmmm." Then she leaned across Luther toward Mossberg. "You sure you're at the right table, Mr. Hats?"

Mossberg grew more and more agitated. He pointed at the placard at the center of the table. "Table Number Nine.

This is Table Number Nine." He tapped his place card. "My *card* says Number Nine. My *shoes* are Number Nine. Everything in my *life* is Number Nine. Of *course* I'm at the right table! What kind of question is that to ask a person?"

Tiger kept her cool. "Well, I don't know what to tell you. Uncle Jack gets very forgetful every now and then."

Mossberg squinted at her. "And I'll tell you something *else*, young lady. You don't look like a Shelda Fleischman to *me*, you don't."

Tiger smiled. "My maiden name was Gottlieb."

Mossberg was not a man easily taken in, and there was a noticeable rise to his voice. "Let me assure you, my St. Louis friends, I know your uncle a lot longer than you do. I know him from Rivington Street. One twenty-one Rivington Street. His mother and my mother went to school together. So if he's sick, I should know about it." He took a deep breath and asked the fateful question. "So how sick *is* he?"

The ball was bouncing around in Luther's court. He drew himself together, hating to tell Mossberg the dire news, yet feeling in all fairness, that he must. "He...ah...called in his accountant."

Mossberg, a businessman, knew what that implied. He straightened stiffly as though being informed of the death of Moshe Dayan. Then he related the grievous information to his wife. "Jack Bergman is very sick."

Mrs. Mossberg shook her head and went, "Oh, tsk-tsk-tsk."

And Mr. Mossberg told her the rest. "Called in his accountant."

"Tsk-tsk-tsk, oh."

The pall that descended upon the Mossbergs lay there

throughout the remainder of the meal, including coffee and mints, giving Luther and Tiger ample time to finish their gluttony, dab their lips with double damask, and turn to listen to the Pledge Taker at the rostrum doing his stuff.

The Pledge Taker was a round man with red hair and great enthusiasm. He was perspiring heavily and was cheered when he removed his dinner jacket, tugged open his tie, and rolled up his sleeves. "All right, gang," he chortled, "we're moving along very well, forging ahead. We are now, if my figuring is correct"—he raised his fist like a cheerleader—"over the one-hundred-thousand-dollar mark!"

The crowd applauded as though Abe Ribicoff had just been announced the President-elect of the U.S.A.

The Pledge Taker spat imaginary spit into his palms, rubbed them together, and exhorted the crowd. "So let's keep the ball rolling. And I think that what we need now is a really big pledge. No more penny-ante, but really big." He went into his world-famous impression of Ed Sullivan. "A really big." And the guests howled with laughter because it sounded more like Sam Levinson. Thus encouraged, the Pledge Taker plowed on. "So far our biggest single pledge is seventy-five hundred dollars. Can't we do better than that? Not to diminish Sam Greenberg's seventy-five-hundred-dollar pledge, but are we gonna let it stop there?" He saw a hand shoot up in the back. "Ah! Back there! Table Number Nine! Yes? And let's really, really hear it!"

Luther stood up magnanimously, nodding to all and beaming an irresistible smile to the people at his table. For the truth was, when Luther smiled, the world was his. The world and all within it were his, forever, and further, and even longer, and double that. He faced the Pledge Taker and called out his pledge in a homey Midwestern manner, confidently but ingratiatingly. "Ten thousand dollars from Mr. and Mrs. Jack Bergman."

There followed a ten-minute round of screaming applause, during which time Tiger stood and kissed Luther as though he had won an Academy Award. Others at Table No. Nine rose and congratulated him, for he was one of theirs, and theirs was now the premier table at the banquet. To hell with Sam Greenberg and Table No. Five! This was Jack Bergman and Table No. Nine! So hooray!

As for Mossberg Hats, he turned to his wife, and suppressing the rising lump in his throat and with tears forming in his eyes, he said of his old friend from Rivington Street, "From the grave he still gives."

And Mrs. Mossberg said, "Oh, tsk-tsk-tsk," only with more feeling than she had ever endowed the words with before.

It was a monumental moment all the way around. And the cheering and applause sustained until the orchestra leader received an invisible directive from some higher source to play, as only he could, a throbbing mambo.

Even as they danced their version of the mambo, and then the cha-cha, and then the merengue, Luther and Tiger could not avoid the congratulatory smiles, comments, and handclasps of other dancers. They were the undeniable hits of the evening, and they reveled in every moment of it, as who wouldn't? And they were pleased to the eyeballs that they had proved so helpful in forwarding so worthy a cause.

But back at the immortalized Table No. Nine, Mr. and Mrs. Mossberg were standing and chatting heatedly with another couple that had just arrived—Mr. and Mrs. Jack

Bergman, a decent enough pair whose car had blown a tire coming down the West Side Highway, causing them to be so dreadfully late at so vital an occasion.

Jack Bergman, upon hearing of his large pledge, bellowed, "What are you talking about, Mossberg? What ten-thousand-dollar pledge? With the state my business is in, I couldn't pledge a bum check."

Mossberg was no longer sure of anything. "But your nephew—he pledged it in your name."

"My nephew can't even *spell* my name. Besides, he's in Chicago."

"This is your nephew from St. Louis."

"I have no nephew in St. Louis. Say, what is this?" Then he looked down at the used utensils and dirty dishes, and he picked up the place cards with his and his wife's name clearly on them, and he looked at the placard with the big number nine on it. "This is Table Number Nine, no? And my card says Number Nine, right? So what's going on around here?"

The citizens of Table No. Nine, though disappointed that their fame was swiftly flying, began to put two and two together and got fraud. Mossberg moved closer to Bergman. "Jack, something fishy is going on here."

Bergman put it more plainly. "You bet your ass it is. I paid five hundred dollars for these plates, and all that's left on them is a design." He looked at his wife, who, like Mrs. Mossberg, was beginning to nod her head in the Orthodox incantation "Tsk-tsk-tsk."

Mossberg spoke again, gradually arriving at an irrefutable conclusion. "Jack, you don't have a nephew from St. Louis named Seymour Fleischman, do you?"

"The only man I know from St. Louis is Stan Musial. And

unless he changed his name, he's no Seymour Fleischman."

"Nor does he have a wife named Shelda, does he?"

"Stan Musial?"

"Shelda Fleischman."

"Who?"

"Your nephew Seymour."

"I *have* no nephew Seymour! Mossberg, if this is your idea of a hilarious joke—"

Mossberg said no more. He just squinted his eyes and swiveled them in a slow traverse of the dance floor, like a U-boat commander with forward tubes ready. Mrs. Mossberg stood beside him, looking at Mrs. Bergman. Together the two matrons exchanged the clucking sounds of the Brazilian Tsk-Tsk Bird.

Luther and Tiger were returning to Table No. Nine when they saw the ominous tableau taking place between the Mossbergs and the Bergmans. Luther deftly executed a neat right-angle turn, and leading Tiger, he merengued across the dance floor to Exit No. Four. And even as they accelerated their terpsichore so that they more nearly resembled Fred Astaire and Ginger Rogers in a rousing finale, they were patted on their backs by guests who envisioned them as some kind of dancing Jewish millionaires, definitely a new breed, a product of the seventies. Tiger kept dancing, her eye on the exit. Luther did likewise, but also managed to smile and accept the crowd's plaudits. He even contributed a few encouraging remarks of his own. "*Shalom aleichem...* Keep 'em flying...Fuck Egypt."

It was touch and go. Luther and Tiger evaded the fast-closing Mossberg-Bergman combine, who were by then exhorting the guests with: "Stop them! Stop, thief! Stop those Fleischmans!"

Astaire and Rogers segued into the anchor leg of the Olympic 440. They made it to the exit, reaching eventual freedom but by devious means—that is, climbing the fire stairs two flights, then descending to earth via the service elevator some forty-five minutes later. By default, Sam Greenberg's pledge held up as the highest of the evening.

3

Luther's pad was large and white and pleasant, with high ceilings and beams and trimmings; it was in an old but well-kept building. The furniture was serviceably spartan, and yet there were a few things—some touches and pieces—that had obviously been selected with affection and set about the apartment with taste. The building was a walk-up brownstone in the East Sixties.

Luther was at his worktable, involved in his hobby, the collection and repair of old toys, most of which were of the Victorian period. The toys barely qualified for the term "antique" because most of them were little more than throwaways: a doll, a tangled marionette, a miniature wrought-iron horse and wagon with a decapitated driver. Still, Luther lavished great attention upon these discarded articles of another time. He was good at it. He could make them sit up, and smile, and look happy and new. It was more than he could do for Tiger.

Tiger was off in another area of the sprawling apartment,

uninvolved with anything in particular, but *aware*. Aware of the weird emptiness to their relationship, the undefined anxiety that always seemed to sweep over the pair of them whenever they were left to themselves with no third party to play off. And often she could hear the voice of Cool Hand Luke: "What we have here is a failure to communicate." They were not good at being alone with each other. And outside of an occasional game of Monopoly, which Luther was gradually cannibalizing by giving away the Take a Chance and Community Chest cards, they seldom even sat opposite each other in the apartment, except at an occasional breakfast.

She glanced over at Luther, who seemed fifty yards away. He looked like a Belgian diamond cutter, hunched over his workbench, performing major surgery on a gem smuggled in from Lisbon. He was almost thirty years old, but he was also seven. He was also a hundred and ninety-three. He was enigmatic, elemental, explosive, unrealistic, and unpredictable. He operated on whim and instinct. He was crafty and could fire a dancing smile without reason and it would melt steel. Yet he *always* had reasons; she just never knew what they were. He was open, attractive, physical. And selfish, and narrow, and mad. He was Luther. One of a kind. An original. And there'd be no more of him passing by. He was Luther the First, Luther the Last, Luther the Only.

She thought about herself and what she was and why. With proper humility she could still believe that she was intelligent and intuitive. Thoughtful and nonexplosive. Not apt to make quick decisions and less apt to change course. She was vulnerable, very. Yes, and pretty. A little to the thin, and a mite to the minus in the bust, but pretty. And she was easily as bright as Luther. No, damn it, brighter. And she was also in possession of her proper senses. Yet if all that were really true, then why was she without ballast and purpose and direction? Unable to function except as the tail to Luther's kite? It was a puzzlement compounded by self-deception. It was also painful and a bore.

She looked out the window at the cars going by five floors below. What if she could *be* in one of them? That one. No, that one. Where would it take her? How many cars would stop and pick her up if she did the Claudette Colbert bit with the skirt raising? One out of four? Five? If she yanked her skirt higher, how many? If she put her skirt so high over her head that she couldn't see at all—and if she just stood there as a pair of legs—how many people? She had good legs. In proportion to the rest of her body they were long. And willowy. And well shaped. Slender ankles, tapering calves. How many cars would stop at the sight of her bare gams? Perhaps three out of five. Perhaps also a police car.

It was all an absurd train of thought. And yet, in a sense, wasn't that how she had met Luther? At that absurd party of…what was his name? Pothead Artie. She had been doing her usual bit of sitting in a corner, combing her hair like Rapunzel, when Luther came over and held out his hand and said, "Take my hand." And she took it. And she left with him, never even having exchanged one word with him. Not knowing, really, whether he sounded like Tiny Tim or Lee Marvin. And she went with him, to his pad, here. And they went to bed as if they'd been doing it forever. And because it was so damned impersonal, she stayed. And that was close to a year ago. And they'd been meandering through life ever since, establishing a life rhythm that few people ever achieved and even fewer were born with. It was safe with Luther. He took care of her. He fed her, and clothed her, and loved her. He'd kill for her. She knew all that, but there was a small clock ticking and growing louder. And she wondered when it would go off and what it would signal. Probably that it was time for her to be taken away and locked up. Then she could sit in a corner in a cell somewhere and comb her hair until it all came out. Hello, Mother. Hi, Dad. You came to see me, how nice. Yes, I'm fine. See my nice hair? See how I comb my nice hair? Isn't my nice hair pretty? See daughter comb her pretty nice hair.

Luther fixed the wheel on the little wrought-iron wagon, and it rolled again as in days of yore, though the headless rider would never see it. "Ha!" exclaimed Luther. "Ha! I have invented the—what shall I call it? The *wheel!* Ha!"

Tiger could only smile because it was now the Children's Hour. She came over to him and stood behind his chair, running her fingers down his shoulders and across as much of his chest as she could span. Then she rested her chin in the thick hair on his head until all the world was a jungle movie. They hadn't really said a word to each other since escaping the UJA. "Luther? How do you think Jack Bergman feels about pledging all that money?"

Luther squirted oil onto the little iron wheel. "Some men are born to greatness; others have it thrust upon them."

"He's some fast runner."

"We're faster."

"Certainly was a fine meal. And you fit in so well. You sure you're not Jewish?"

"It's always possible. Maybe my parents lied to me about my circumcision. Maybe it *wasn't* an accident."

She looked over his head and down at the wagon that he was pushing back and forth. "You fixed it."

"Yes. If I push it, I can get a thousand miles to the gallon."

"Or if you only drive it downhill."

"Yeah. That'd do it."

Her hands were all about him, twin snakes on an oak trunk, and she nibbled at his ears and kissed the nape of his neck and generally sent out the signal that she was at home and was receiving callers.

Luther gave the little wagon a short shove, and it rolled the length of his worktable, where it socked into a fat Raggedy Ann Doll that was still recuperating from a frontal lobotomy. "Officer," he said, "get the number of that wagon. And fireman, save my child." Then he stood up; and standing behind him with her hands still clasped about his neck, she was astounded to see her feet come off the floor. She felt like a knapsack. He removed the knapsack, turning her in midair, never letting her toes touch earth, and he kissed her.

It was a sweet kiss, innocent, yet intimate. And it triggered that response in her that she wanted to have triggered. She became more fervent as his arms closed more tightly about her. It was just possible, she thought, that she might never come down. And that would be fine. But the kiss suspiciously transformed into something else, something sinister and unsettling. Still holding her, Luther withdrew his mouth from hers and looked into her face with widening eyes. She could see the pupils dilating, the eyeballs just this side of spinning. His brow slowly curled into an evil knot. A bizarre grimace took shape upon his face, his lips turning under, baring sharp and threatening teeth.

Tiger turned almost rigid as she watched him go through the horrible metamorphosis. And she gasped when the drool escaped from the corner of his mouth. Then his face swooped slowly down, a lazy vulture, and his mouth clamped tightly on her neck, and she felt the sucking there. She knew that her pulsating jugular was exposed, and she could feel his teeth searching out its dimensions. She knew that she was dying. She could feel the blood rushing through the rising purple vein. Slowly his mouth leeched suckingly harder to her lifeline, and she went limp, her eyes frozen open, staring unblinkingly at the white shimmying ceiling. She felt herself being lowered to the floor. Gently, gently. He let her slide from his arms and from his mouth.

She lay on the floor, supine and seemingly lifeless, her breath totally suspended. He knelt beside her and closely examined the red welt on her neck with a curious, yet professional demeanor. And when he spoke, his voice was tinged with the timbre of dispassionate science. "Odd," he said, "no signs of violence except for these two almost invisible needlelike punctures. I suspect that what we're dealing with here is beyond the ken of science."

Tiger could say nothing. She still stared with uncomprehending eyes. Slowly her breathing returned, in short spastic puffs at first, then gradually in long and liquidy gasps. It took her a bare few moments more to realize that Luther had only been doing a shtik.

Seeing the terror still lingering about her, Luther smiled his usual ingratiating beacon and caressed the fair face and the lovely hair. He hadn't intended to frighten her to that degree. "Hi," he said. "I love you."

The fear over, the tears came. Torrents and gushes, cascades and rushes. She should have known. And she clutched at him as though he had just saved her from some dragon. She clutched at him hard, pulling him down upon her. And she thought, how lovely. All the toys on his shelf could watch them make love. How very special. How very much like Christmas Eve in Santa's Workshop. Hey, toys, watch this. Watch and learn. For if you can someday do what we are now doing, it will mark the beginning of a wondrous new era in the development of educational toys and in the progression of creative playthings. Watch me, little dolls. Watch, you soldiers and cowboys and teddy bears. See the loving. See Luther make love to Tiger. Quick, Luther, quick. Come, Tiger, come.

She knew that he watched over her at night. Even in her sleep she could feel him there, lying on his side, studying her. Once, when she woke up somewhere before dawn, it was because he was running his big palm gently through her hair. He told her that it was okay, to go back to sleep, he was guarding her. She asked him, "Against what?" And he said, "Against the dybbuks inside you—the ones trying to take over." To which she said, "I have no dybbuks, you dope." And he went on to say, "Everyone has dybbuks. But it doesn't matter. I don't need much sleep. Besides, it's nice to lie beside the girl you love and listen to her breathe and know, that if anything comes, you'll protect her from it. When a woman sleeps, that's when she's a child and needs caring. Also, nutsy, if you want to get mathematical about it, if we spend one-third of our lives asleep, that makes you, when you're asleep, a little more than six years old, and six-year-olds need caring. Not until you're ninety should you sleep without someone watching. It's too risky." The following morning, of course, he denied ever having made such a speech to her. He made a similar speech a week later, and a similar denial. So she never mentioned it again or asked why he watched over her, mostly because she liked it.

4

They certainly enjoyed their bacon and eggs the next morning. They certainly did. After a full night of love-making, Luther could usually consume half his weight in calories, and that morning was no exception. As for Tiger, she, too, laid into the breakfast goodies if for no other reason than to replace the weight that Luther had "loved" off her during the night. She had an uncanny sense of just how much weight she lost in any given love session. And because of the high passions involved, last night, by her calculations, had been a rousing three-pounder. So she waded into breakfast as would a host of locusts, lest her weight fall below her usual nifty 107 pounds.

"Mmmmm," said Luther. "Good bacon."

"Ummmmm, yes," said Tiger. "Delicious. And no mess."

The demonstrator was very pleased and continued his spiel. "Yes, and it all works on high frequency sound waves. No grease, no waiting. Just forty-eight seconds for the bacon and ten seconds for the eggs."

The other people standing around in Bloomingdale's epicurean department seemed impressed with the demonstration. But Luther and Tiger, by dint of having placed themselves strategically in the crowd's forefront, were the only ones imbibing of the breakfast fare. They stood there, balancing their little plates, and smacking their little lips, and generally enjoying their little repast while the demonstrator continued to extoll the efficacies of the jim-dandy little sonic oven. "Yes, indeed…no modern kitchen can really consider itself complete without this high-speed futuristic cooker." The demonstrator, obviously an out-of-work actor, was reveling in his moment in the sun. So he turned to Luther and Tiger and went into his Great Dunninger routine. "Now then, for the record, you two have never seen me before." He smiled and winked at the good-natured crowd, who, no doubt, were appreciating his fine performance.

"True," said Luther, and Tiger nodded her agreement.

"Neither of you is in the employ of Bloomingdale's," said the demonstrator, building his foolproof case.

"No, sir. We are not."

"There is no collusion. You are not shills?"

"No, sir."

"You just wandered into Bloomingdale's this morning and kindly consented to be guinea pigs, is that correct?" The demonstrator had switched from Dunninger to Clarence Darrow.

"Correct."

"And what, then, is your conclusion?"

Luther was everything that Bloomingdale's had ever dreamed of. "My conclusion is—that I have never tasted bacon this crisp without its being dry and lifeless. There's no curled-up edges, no loss of flavor…"

He looked at Tiger, and she took that as her smiling cue. "And the eggs are perfect," she said. "Delicate and tasty and barnyard fresh."

The demonstrator, out of his mind with the performances of his cast, closed in for his dramatic climax. "And would you like to know exactly how much this incredible little oven costs? Would you care to hazard a guess?"

Luther did not flinch at the hazard. "Eight thousand dollars and twenty-three cents."

Tiger added, "Plus tax."

The demonstrator, a man who had not studied with Lee Strasberg without results, gave the world the correct figure. "Only four hundred ninety-nine dollars and ninety-five cents!"

Luther expressed facial amazement and exhaled a gasp of shock. Then he pulled himself together, and clapping his hands as though sealing a bargain, he announced, "Jesus Christ, I have to have one."

Tiger was surprised. It served her right for ever assuming that Luther knew when it was time to quit. All she could do now was watch and see how the situation would develop.

The demonstrator was tickled out of his skull. He whipped out his order pad, probably from up his sleeve, and drew out a pencil as if it were the fastest Eberhard Faber in the West. "And the name, please?"

Tiger waited to hear what the name would be. Luther did not back off as he stated it for all mankind to hear. "Mr. Jack Bergman."

Bong. Tiger knew that they had passed the point of no

return. All that could follow would be disaster. She gently tugged at Luther's sleeve, like a child indicating to Daddy that it was time to cut out. Luther gave ground grudgingly, still addressing the demonstrator as he was being pulled away by Tiger. "Put a card in, please. To Uncle Jack, with lavish and idiotic affection, from Seymour and Shelda and all the gang at Mossberg Hats."

The demonstrator had run out of script. He was watching his life, luck, and commission, all leaving together, backward. "But—"

Tiger tugged Luther farther and farther away from the confused demonstrator and the equally baffled crowd. She led him straight and cool, neither fast nor slow, but most assuredly away. They moved through another little area in the epicurean department. The bakery section, where little fresh-baked cookies lay cooling on a counter, delectably, as in a Tom Sawyer movie, as though just placed there by Aunt Polly. Luther inhaled and stopped short. And Tiger's legs kept going a few steps farther, climbing only on air.

Luther smiled at the chubby lady baker who looked like one of the Campbell Kids grown up. "Hi," he said as he reached over with one of his paws and picked up three cookies in one move. "Mmmmm," he said. "Good. And real butter, too."

"Yes, sir," she said. "And only a dollar ninety-five a pound." Everybody was selling in Bloomingdale's. Hardly the Christmas spirit. But then it was hardly Christmas. It was October.

Luther filled his pockets with cookies as the chubby lady watched with disbelief. "Don't you want me to...put them in a box?"

"Oh, no," said Luther. "Don't bother. I'm not paying." And he felt Tiger's tug on his sleeve, and he moved along after her, stopping only to shout back to the stove demonstrator. "And put in three dozen of these fine and tasty cookies! Jack Bergman! It's in the garment center somewhere! They'll know!"

Tiger tugged again, and they moved along. They turned a corner and bumped into a woman shopper who was intensely examining an electric coffeepot. Luther folded his hands behind his back and immediately became a floorwalker. "Yes? May I help you?"

The woman looked up at him and brandished the pot. "How much is this? It doesn't say."

Tiger leaned against a counter and sighed skyward as Luther professionally examined the coffeepot. "Hmmmm," he said. "Ah, yes. It's eleven ninety-five. But for you, because it's Arbor Day—six fifty." He placed the pot back into her surprised hands. "You see," he said, smiling, "it's really a piece of crap." He felt Tiger's tug and was soon moving down the aisle. A few yards, and he turned back to the lady shopper and called out, "At a hundred and fifty-five degrees it self-destructs!" The lady dropped the coffee pot and went immediately to the complaint department.

Luther and Tiger finally left the department store. But not until Luther had autographed Irwin Shaw's name on three separate copies of Norman Mailer's latest novel much to the giggly satisfaction of a trio of New Rochelle matrons to whom he had identified himself as Truman Capote. Also, at the perfume counter, he asked to have three gallons of Réplique shipped quickly to the New York Knickerbocker locker room, and before the next game, please. In the infants' section he hastily instructed the saleslady immediately to ship eight cribs to the Olesky octuplets in Manitoba, charging the whole thing to *Cosmopolitan* magazine, which, he said, had just acquired the rights to at least five of the kids, though, as far as he knew, *Life* magazine owned the other three, but they'd all work it out somehow.

Bloomingdale's was not to be the same for some time. It was the third time that year that the Phantom Imbecile had struck, and they were hard at work checking his fingerprints with the FBI from the *last* time when he hit them again. That afternoon Bloomingdale's checked with Macy's and Gimbels but received no cooperation, though they thought they heard laughter on the other end of the line.

Luther and Tiger romped happily down Lexington Avenue, leaving Bloomingdale's to heaven. It was a glittering day, and they both felt good, finishing up their hearty breakfast with cookies that came endlessly from Luther's large pockets.

They walked through the world like that almost every day, with other people and other sounds floating all about them like blurred pastiches—but they were never touched by anything outside their own tiny perimeter. Luther and Tiger belonged only to each other, and nothing else was allowed in. Nor did anything else try. People who bumped people never bumped Luther and Tiger. Vehicles that intimidated all life never threatened them. Things that fell from windows, cranes that toppled, gas mains that burst, arms that broke, hearts that attacked—none of these presented the slightest danger to Luther and Tiger. For they had their invisible shield, and beneath it, they wore their enchanted garments, and within those folds they bore their exalted love. And in all such moments Tiger could feel the power of him, tall and tousled and slightly daft. King of the hill. Lord of the manor. Cock of the walk. Christ at large on Halloween Night, tweaking noses, pulling legs, tricking and treating, but hurting no one.

The drugstore loomed up as an oasis, like the only place in town, like the last train out of Istanbul. Tiger felt Luther stiffen, and when she looked up into his face, she could actually see the brazen idea festering.

Luther removed his jacket and handed it to Tiger as though she were his valet. Then he rolled up his sleeves, and Tiger looked round, wondering who it was he was going to fight. There was no one, of course. Only Luther, looking through the glass door of the drugstore at the action beyond. And when Tiger looked, too, she found herself kissed gently upon the head. And when she turned her face up, the better to receive his kisses, he was already moving through the doorway. She was always one step behind him. It was her lot. She was forever doomed to be a split-second post-Luther. Nor was there any way in which to anticipate his actions.

So she remained outside the drugstore, hugging his jacket. From her vantage point, allowing for reflections, Tiger could still see fairly well through the glass door. At the eating counter sat New Yorkers of the morning, gobbling coffee and Danish just prior to turning themselves in at their offices. And behind the long counter a half dozen white-shirted countermen went frenetically about their business. They were harassed, confused, and vitally busy, involved with orders and questions from customers whose faces were long and whose tempers were short. So immersed in their activity were the countermen that they didn't notice their number swell by one—the tall man in the white shirt with the rolled-up sleeves, direct to Whalen's, courtesy of Central Casting. Needless to say, Tiger did not care for the situation that Luther had so nonchalantly stepped himself into. The getting there was half the fun. The getting back would be another kind of journey.

Luther swung into action, and Tiger gulped at his gall. He grabbed a rag and polished the counter and generally moved about in the same frenzied patterns as did the other countermen. He even deigned to shout out a few orders to the unseen chef in the back. In the clatter and the clamor none of his orders was heard. But that didn't dissuade him. "Burn one! BT. down, kill the gravy, it's to go!"…"One double garlic malt, easy on the chutney!"…"Still waiting for my liverburger, Marlene!"

His directives mingled with other hoarse orders, and no one questioned the sanity of *any* of them. But it made him feel a part of the team, and Luther liked that. He believed in camaraderie on the job. And since the six others were yelling at the kitchen, then by gum, he'd do it, too. The important part of the entire maneuver he carried off with Lutherian style. For as he polished the countertop, he also pocketed the tips, slyly sliding the coins across the counter toward his belly, allowing them to plop into his unobserved palm, which then introduced them to his pocket. And all the while he slowly worked his way from the far end of the counter back toward the doorway, beyond which he could see Tiger's openmouthed face pressed against the window.

"Pastrami lean, on white bread, with mayo!" He grimaced as he ordered that one because it was such a godawful combination, and he looked around at the customers as if to say, "Which one of you dum-dums ordered that?"

One of the countermen, a scarred ex-sailor with hairy tattoos and heavy muscles, was looking at Luther and checking him out because he wasn't sure that he'd seen him there before. He was posted between Luther and the door, and he stopped what he was doing and watched and waited as Luther came polishing toward him. He was a menacing man with a frazzled cigarette dangling from his swarthy face, the smoke spiraling up into his squinty eyes already swollen from the boozy night before.

Tiger noticed the man immediately. She watched him plant his feet and place his big hands on his hips, and she feared that the jig was up and that Luther would shortly be confronted with his dishonesty and leniently punished with mere death. She hated whenever Luther put himself into such jeopardy. It wasn't any fun when he did that. It frightened her. And she could feel her heart pumping, and she had trouble gathering oxygen. She raised one finger in an effort to gain Luther's attention. More she could not do.

Luther could not have really seen the powerful torso in his path. And yet he somehow knew that the man was there. And without a moment's hesitation and without even looking to see if the man was large or small or dead or alive or a duck, Luther squeezed by and addressed the man very *sotto voce.* "Dowse the butt. Health inspector."

The big counterman, suddenly guilty and equally fearful, whipped the cigarette from his ugly mouth, pulling part of his lip with it. Then, doubling up out of sight, he shoved the butt hissingly into someone's upcoming orange juice. And, in that split second of measured time, Luther the Wisp was past him. And in the *next* split second Luther was out the door.

Tiger had his jacket ready; there was not a moment to lose. She held it toward him, and he thrust both arms into it, and they were on their way, turning a corner, vanishing.

Tiger, breathless and angry, chastised him for his stupid gambit. But he only laughed as, with great pride, he showed her his pocketful of coins. She looked into his oversized pocket (Luther had oversized pockets for professional reasons) and witnessed the collection. Had they been doubloons, they'd both have been wealthy. But Tiger only grew more and more upset, whereas Luther, not choosing to argue the point, merely steered her farther up the street, and even as she was scolding him, he whisked her into a mod jewelry shop.

When they emerged, Tiger had a cheap ring for each finger. Her hands were so heavy that she could barely raise the rings to the sun to see just how cheap the glass was. Nor could she touch her fingers together. They remained spread, like a cat's, and her hands dangled helplessly at her side as though they had originally belonged to a much larger person. For all his work, Luther had only his smile. He had squandered his hard-earned booty on the pretty wench, but it had seemingly produced results. For if she had not truly forgiven him his crime, she had, at least for the moment, forgotten it in a blaze of gaudy jewelry. He was sure it was not too different in Tortuga and Port Royal, years ago when Captain Morgan and his men tossed trinkets to strumpets and then sailed away for more. He put his big arm about her and gathered her to his side. Once again he had risked all for a pretty girl, but such a pretty girl.

5

The sun was high and warm over Central Park. It was the noon to two break in the day, and many office workers took to the park benches just to sit and contemplate trees. Luther and Tiger strolled along, quite the laconic couple, appreciating nature and generally approving of October, which still had a dash of summer in its veins. Luther was whistling his favorite song, "The Star-Spangled Banner," and it never ceased to amaze Tiger that the national anthem was the only song he concerned himself with in his more meditative moments. He was either a patriot or a put-down artist. Whichever, he was a good whistler.

They walked the twisting paths, and Tiger was troubled. It had been occurring to her more and more frequently that by staying with Luther, she was going nowhere. Not that she minded living only for the present. She didn't. It was crazily unique, especially when superimposed on her Protestant background, which, very early on, had pointed her always to the future, so much so that she never really remembered enjoying anything along the way. Always the future, the future. Hurry up and get there. And when you've gotten there, take a nice look around and feel very satisfied that you've lived by the Protestant ethic, and once you've done that...die.

Still, living with Luther smacked of waste. Luther was wasting. He was a wastrel and a wasting waster. Surely he was capable of doing many things well. He was good with his hands—why was he not an artist or a sculptor? Or an architect or an engineer? He was open and verbal and glib, and possessed such a glittering personality—why wasn't he a vice-president somewhere? He was inventive and original—he could be a writer, a philosopher, a television personality. What was Johnny Carson before they put a camera on him? Or Dick Cavett, for that matter? Luther could be many things, anything. Yet he chose to be nothing. He could, but he wouldn't. He was but he wasn't. And it all rose up in her throat until Tiger found herself verbalizing her concern. "You play so many parts that sometimes I forget who you are."

"They call me Clark Kent."

"And most of the time I never even know who it is who's making love to me."

"Oh. That's Captain Marvel."

Comic books, she thought. That was his frame of reference. It bugged her so, but she knew to keep it light if her point was to be made. "Don't you think it shows an alarming lack of self-confidence never to be yourself?"

"Yes." He was not being drawn in.

"Then why can't you *be* yourself every once in a while?"

"I'll try it Thursday." And he thought on it deeply. "Who

do you suppose I am?"

"Luther, *please*—"

"Luther! Right. *That's* who I am." And he snapped his fingers. "Must try to remember."

"Okay, forget it. You want to be a little boy? Fine. Want to wet your pants? Fine. I don't care. I really don't." She really did.

He put his arm about her, and she had to walk along the path as though leaning against a moving building. "Listen, nutsy," he said, "open up a man, any man. Open him up and give him air, and do you know what jumps out? A little boy jumps out. Jumps out and yells, 'Hi ho, Silver.' Everything else after that is just an act. That's all it is."

"Okay. I don't care. I really don't." She was sulking. A real fine sulk. Complete with lower lip pouting and eyes cast at the points of her shoes. The classic sulk.

They approached a bench where three junior executive types sat, none of them knowing the other two, and so there was a separation on the bench between all three. Luther was still explaining to Tiger. "Just an act. The deep voice, the money in the bank"—he pointed to the shined shoes of the first man—"the shined shoes"—he pointed to the magazine that the second man was reading—"*Newsweek* magazine, it's all an act. Take any man." He stopped at the third man, who looked up disbelievingly. "Take *this* man." Luther was making no effort to modulate his voice, and to the people in the vicinity it sounded as though he were making a speech. He pointed at the third man, his finger practically on the man's nose. "What he'd *really* like to do is kick over his job and jerk off for forty hours a week. Plus overtime. Right?" The man started to say something, but Luther spoke first.

"Right." Then he pulled Tiger farther along the path, and she was perfectly mortified. As was the third young executive, who never moved at all. Partly because he knew that it didn't happen. But mostly because he knew it was true.

Tiger loved Luther's insane capers. Still, because of her upbringing, she was often embarrassed by the things he'd say and do. And many times she'd hear her mother's voice screaming in the wake of one of Luther's bits. As for the family minister, she always pictured *him* toppling from the pulpit and getting sucked into the massive organ, emerging only as an F# in the following hymn.

Soon they came upon two old men playing chess. A few other people sat around on nearby benches, only half-interested in the cerebral confrontation.

Luther indicated to Tiger that she was to hold her ground. He, to the contrary, walked up to the two ancient combatants. Then he knelt between them, his eyes at chess-board level, and the two old men didn't know what to make of him, so they pretty much ignored him. Luther, meantime, surveyed the chess pieces like a huge aardvark checking out an ant colony. Ultimately he looked up and smiled engagingly, first at one old man and then at the other. And then he addressed both of them as though they were children. "Is this a way?"

The two men didn't know what to make of that observation, so they stopped playing and listened to the rest of what the aardvark had to say.

"Must there always be a winner?" Luther asked. "Isn't that what's really wrong with the world today? I ask you— what would happen if there were no leaders?" With that Luther calmly removed the two kings from the chessboard.

"There"—he smiled—"now there's no longer any reason for going on with it, is there?" Luther stood and addressed the other people, who by then were all ears. "Let there no more killing." He raised his hands in benign benediction. "Let there be only peace. And let it be known that it started here, today, in this park, on this bench, with these two wise men." He laid a hand on the shoulder of one of the old players. His other hand he laid over his own heart. "Bless you both. The President will be pleased."

Luther walked away as he imagined Mark Antony would have done, leaving the two players, a governess and her baby, two unemployed bookkeepers, three squirrels, and some pigeons to reflect on the profoundness of his words. Then, taking Tiger's arm sweetly, he walked with her and filled in the true meaning of it all. "And the moral of the story is: There is no reason for any man to play chess...unless...he's too old to jerk off."

They walked along. And shortly Luther was off into one of his patented philosophical monologues. Tiger could do nothing but listen, and nod, and say "Mmmmmm."

"Chess is an astounding game because it's the truest expression of womankind's urge to either be in total command or kill. I mean, the whole thing is over when the king buys it, and along the way, everyone else is fucked. The knights have short careers and usually get it up the ass from management. The bishops, Lord bless 'em, they're pretty fascinating because they still reflect the church of the Middle Ages, always playing all the angles and *only* the angles. Ah, but for true sexual sagacity, I give you *the queen*. For it's the queen who does the real damage. Talk about your Women's Lib, where is the female more in charge than on a chessboard? The stupid king, he's a leadfoot who seldom moves too far from his castle because that's where the bank comes for the mortgage payments. Whereas the queen, ah, the queen—she's out swinging all over the kingdom, chewing up pawns, defrocking bishops, fellating knights, and generally terrorizing the castles, of which she has two, one in Grosse Point and one in Bermuda. And worst of all, the queen is always glamming eyes on the other king, a nice royal fellow who's home alone because his own wife is off screwing everyone in Bangor, Maine. And watch how often, when a queen is fucked, how it's a knight who slimies up to her and sticks it in her because she's left a crooked door open and let him zigzag in. And then, instead of crying with shame, she simply rams back at the big stallion and says, 'Game's over. My place or yours?' The reason I prefer checkers is that checkers is so much more democratic. In checkers a guy can *become* a king by his own efforts, rather than, as in chess, having to be *born* a king. Also, the real thrill in checkers is in jumping one another, quickly and without heavy plotting. The supreme kick being a triple jump in which, because you've played it so cool, you're screwing three of the little darlings on one bed in the Henry Hudson Hotel. But what I really like best is Monopoly because, in Monopoly, if you're busted, you can get out of jail for just fifty bucks, and because, every time you pass the place where it all started, Daddy gives you two hundred bucks so's you can get in trouble all over again."

Tiger said "Mmmmm," and they went home.

6

"My check came in today," Luther said. "I'm paid a king's ransom never to set foot in Scarsdale again. I *like* a good healthy father-son relationship like that. Makes a man *proud* to be born with a silver spoon up his ass." He was working on a forlorn doll that had once been a ballerina. In his skillful hands it was fast assuming a second chance. A half-severed leg had been mended almost invisibly, and a new smile was dancing on the doll's sweet patrician face.

Tiger was off by herself in her usual corner, her chin resting on her knees as she gazed out the window at the nothingness of midnight. She was pensive to the point of being completely out of it when a mixed bag of sounds sprung a leak in her mind. They trickled through—sounds of a few years ago, muted and hollow, stumbling over one another in an effort to gain primary attention. Her mother's voice, a bit harsh and a lot urging, as always was first. *"Janice? Janice, are you ready? Freddie is here. He's waiting. Janice, you spend your life in that tub. Janice, do you—."* Her mother's voice was shortly displaced by the mingled voices of the high school cheering squad, of which Tiger was the prettiest, the loudest, and the highest jumper.

> *We've got the team,*
> *We've got the stuff;*
> *Eastern, Eastern—*
> *Rough, rough, rough!*

In the ensuing roar, Dashing Donny McKay took the ball on Eastern's eight and went all the way with it to Michigan State, where he proceeded to not make the varsity and never write to her. Finis to you, Dashing Don, and we're all glad you're captain of the team from Oblivion.

The soothing voice of Dr. Martindale phased in. Sweet old Doc Martindale, Eastern's principal, addressing the oh-so-sober graduating class. *"And it is our hope that, many years from now, should the Class of Sixty-seven ever return, some of us will still be here to greet you. But until that time, we will raise the window high, for Robin wants to fly. We will leave some breadcrumbs on the ledge, in case Robin cares to return…"*

The tear-splattered alma mater came next as she stood up with the others and sang, for the last time, *"Dear school of ours, Dear Eastern High, your loyal sons and daughters know how—"*

"You're strangely silent tonight, my darling." Luther's voice snapped the brittle melody, putting a period on the bittersweet recollections.

Tiger looked up and saw him smiling there. She pulled herself out of her reverie, a thing she was getting quite good at, and she smiled back at him. "Hi." Then she made another typical move, a shrug of self-consciousness that seemed to announce, "You caught me dreaming again, oh, well."

Luther cocked his head quizzically. "All right, nutsy, what is it *this* time?"

"Nothing"—she smiled—"just my entire life passing before me. It'll…pass."

He curled up alongside her, and they looked like two kids first on line, waiting for the circus admission gate to open. "Am *I* in it?"

"No. Sorry."

"How come? Was I out of town?"

She laughed. "Man, you are *always* out of town. You were *born* out of town, and you will *die* out of town."

"You're trying to tell me something."

"No."

"Yes. You're about to launch yourself into another long speech on emotional involvement, followed by some kind of diatribe on commitment."

Tiger was confused by her own thinking, so she laughed because it was better than crying. "Well, I *know* I don't want to commit to *you* because *you* are only seven years old."

"Hark. It comes. The raucous cackle of the Midwestern Love-Me-Bird."

She thought about that, then nodded a kind of half-hearted agreement. "It's a nicer sound than the Scarsdale Screw-You Bird, no?"

"Make your point." He was smiling, and that was maddening because it drew all the venom from her fangs.

"Okay," she said, determined to make good use of the opening. "I think it's that even if I'm *not* loved, I'd like to *feel* loved. And you don't give me that feeling. How's that?"

"Great. It implies that I don't love you. How very Hitler of you to frame it in that manner."

A small pique was building in her temperament. "Does it ever occur to you that—I mean, it occurs to me—that I might just get pregnant. What happens *then?*"

"Occur yourself an abortion."

She got up. "Swell." She hated the fact that she could never draw him into a discussion on anything she felt was important. He was always elusive and disinterested, and it was depressing her to the point where she was having difficulty coping with it. She walked away. But not too far because, if she kept right on going, she knew he wouldn't stop her.

Luther remained by the window, still magnificently sidestepping the facts of their relationship. "Tiger, I have always trusted you. And included in that trust is the trust that you have been regularly taking your pill, I trust."

She faced him calmly because where Luther was concerned, fire was best fought with fire and not ire. "You have every reason to trust me. You sprinkle those pills on everything I eat, including yourself."

"A lovely thought, but an exaggeration."

"I found three of them in my Jello."

"Those were grapes."

"Grapes do not come with instructions."

"The instructions were for the Jello. The last batch you made, if you remember, swelled out so much we had to *shoot* it. And it was *orange*, the least virulent of the species. Damned shame."

Tiger had had enough. "Well, like I said, it's nothing." She was very down and stickily self-pitying. But she didn't care. She felt end-of-the-line and clearly saw that there was no longer any real purpose in staying alive. "Actually, the last three *years* of my life are nothing because...*I'm* nothing."

She was over at her big purse, fingers fumbling in it. "And it shouldn't go on any longer—I don't think." She had her hand on the little vial, and it made her words behave more and more erratically. "And, having carefully thought it over—I find that, when it's all said and done—" The vial felt warm in her hand. She wasn't afraid of it. She wanted it.

Luther looked up. He was alerted to something. He couldn't see exactly what it was that she had taken from her purse. But he was distrustful of her halting words and odd movements.

She tried to be brave, to keep back the tears. She wanted him to see her with a smile on her face so she turned to look at him once more. "Anyway—"

"Tiger?"

She knew exactly what she was doing. She raised the vial toward him, as in a toast. "I hope you won't try to stop me."

He moved toward her, quickly, but not quickly enough.

She tossed her head back and drained the vial and just stood there, looking at Luther, who had stopped in his tracks. She smiled and said, "Oh, well." She smiled again, but it came out as a grimace, and her body jerked, and she seemed to stiffen and recoil. She gasped. Staggered. Coughed. All her unhappiness translated down into this one brief moment of agony. Her fingers curled into a claw. Her body stooped arthritically. She looked at him through wild brown eyes, and she knew she had him. She was giving the son of a bitch two tits for his every tat. "Doctor, I...feel that...I don't know what comes over...and—" She shuffled toward him, bent as a witch, dragging one leg tortuously, her tongue hanging out of her mouth like a drooling hound's.

It hit Luther like a bell. She was doing a bit. Marvelous! He backed away in feigned terror, covering his mouth with a frightened fist. "No! Go back! Back, I say!"

"No escaping me now, Doctor…now that you know my secret." She laughed insanely, and gurgled, and even salivated, all the while moving toward him, her claws practically dragging along the floor like the knuckles of a baboon. Her breath came in fast snorts, as though she were trying to blow sharp pebbles from her nose.

"Faversham!" he warned. "Get hold of yourself! Surely, there's an antidote!"

She kept shuffling toward him, her eyes glowing sheer lunacy, groans coming from the very base of her larynx. "Yes…Something I have to do."

"What? For God's sake, what?"

"I have to ball you."

"Oh, that—"

She was on him like a cat, and he found himself struggling beneath her continuous low growl. Things toppled from tables, and the earth trembled five levels below as she threw her bones on his with Olympian lust. It was love but not quite, for it was far too violent to qualify for the word. It was something else and something apart. Something instigated by Tiger—an urge to inflict hurt, to punish, to end. She was the predator, wrapped about the big wildebeest like a feline clam. Her ankles locked his legs together, holding him properly in place, while her anvil thighs hammered him home. It was near impossible for him to breathe, let alone function. And he wasn't so much a male participant as he was a hapless tool. She clawed him and pounded him with fists of clenched granite. And she bit, and thrashed, and writhed—and none of it was in passion. All of it was born of some lurking drive to kill that which was killing her.

7

Later, or earlier the next morning, the storm had subsided, and they nestled together in the warm aftermath. The tigress had been sated, but the phallus, though flaccid, had won again. She huddled very close to him, her anger spent, replaced by an ambiance of belonging which she knew to be false but which she reveled in just the same. Luther waited until her eyes flickered back to full awareness, and when the clear things revealed that she was fully awake and breathing like a human being once again, he reached over and bestowed upon her the little ballet dancer he had repaired before Rome toppled onto both of them.

Tiger squealed delightedly, for she had believed the little doll to be beyond salvaging. And she thought to herself, how marvelous, she's me. She didn't say it aloud, but then again, maybe she *did*. Because Luther was saying, "Hmmmm. There *is* a resemblance; only...she doesn't wet."

"She's smiling."

"Why not? Blue Cross is paying for everything."

"Well," she said, brazen as a cuspidor, "you fixed *me* up, too."

"Another triumph for Medicare."

"That injection was just what I needed."

"How often do you get those seizures?"

"As often as I can get those injections."

"I see. Well, you mustn't become too reliant on them. The supply may run out."

She was happy. Glad to be alive. Pleased to still be with him. Whatever had been before, and whatever was on the way, none of it could dislodge her dependency on him. Modesty, upbringing, ladylike decorum—all of it went by the boards whenever they made love. He could reduce her to nothing more than a sexual container with just five thrusts of his marvelous member. She could hate him *before*, but she'd love him during and after. And *he* knew it as well as *she* did, so why hide from it? Who was there around to expel her from the convent? "Luther—I love you."

"Ah," he said, twisting his nonexistent mustache, "that makes two of us."

"If I apologize, will you accept?"

"Certainly. What's the apology for?"

"For crowding you."

"Forget it," he said, feeling crowded. "I know I have my shortcomings."

"Shortcomings!" She laughed. "Why, you have more shortcomings than a midget nymphomaniac."

He chuckled with pride. "Very good. I keep forgetting how clever you can be."

"Yes. And me from a family where mother and father are honored and Christianity revered."

He grew stiffly uncomfortable and changed the subject shamelessly. "My darling countess, news has come. News of an unsettling nature."

She said nothing, just watched him get out of bed, bolt naked. He turned to her with grandiose smile and went into his bit as if he were fully attired in noble raiment. "France has fallen. Our comrades are in shackles." He raised one finger as though brandishing a royal scepter. "But *one* has escaped. One near and dear to me."

She went along with the male Godiva. "And his name, pray tell?"

"Fat Chance."

"Pardon?" She was instantly nonplussed. Was he putting her down? Or worse, was he deliberately confusing her? Not letting her get too close to him?

"That's his name. Theodore 'Fat' Chance. Theodore, after his father. Fat, after his belly."

"Fat Chance."

"Yes. Somehow he evaded the vile English trap, and already he's on his way…here."

"Here."

"Yes."

"To live."

"Yes," and he turned smilingly sincere. "He's an old friend. An accountant who's fallen on hard times and…he's been evicted from his pad and I bumped into him in the A&P, where he was stealing bouillon cubes and I said, 'Fat, come and stay with us.'"

"For how long?"

"For the time being." He turned away and, evidently feeling naked, slipped into his robe while adding, "Starting tomorrow." Then he picked up his guitar and sat down with it and acted as if he had never mentioned Fat Chance at all. "Here's an old sea chanty my father wrote for me the night I was conceived. It was first played on my mother's labia, and nine months later, it was performed in concert on our common umbilical cord. As I recall, it went something like this:

> I hope you're a girl,
>   because if you're not;
> I can't name you Florence,
>   or Helen, or Spot.

He played and sang with a frightening ease, but was very careful not to look at Tiger. Cued by his casual manner, Tiger silently acknowledged that a new phase in their relationship had begun. The Age of Zigzag. It would come in obliquely, and it would settle in devious mosaics. It would bewilder and pain for a while before eventually giving way to a more final ending, which was no doubt already in the wind. And she trembled in the smell of it, for she realized that, as always, she would be powerless in the face of change and hopeless in the wake of parting. Still, there was always the possibility that it was exactly as Luther had stated it, a coincidental meeting in the A&P with an old friend. Fat chance.

8

Tiger could see that Fat had been aptly dubbed. He was Fat. Fat like a cherubic Buddha. Squat and bottom-heavy and somewhat pear-shaped, he was in his mid-twenties and still growing, sideways. He was neatly, if not fastidiously, dressed in what could only be described as Altoona Baroque. He showed no outward signs of poverty, yet possessed no inward qualities of great breeding. He was a pleasant enough type, soft-spoken—even subdued. Still, even as he smiled at her, Tiger couldn't help recalling that there was a subsurface to every iceberg, and a dark side to the moon, and thorns to the rose, and seeds to the grape, and rats in the basement of even the finest houses. Whose rat and what basement Fat had come from remained to be seen.

Luther was at the far end of his apartment, fussing with a toy that had seen better days, while Fat stood facing Tiger, his valises at his side. He seemed genuinely apologetic. "I'm sure it's an imposition, but I guess it couldn't be helped. I have no place to stay and"—he had to reach for the words, and what he came up with sounded suspiciously like a repetition of something Tiger had heard the night before—"having fallen upon hard times…so—" He shot his small shoulders into an upward shrug, looking like a turtle retreating. And when he let them come down, all his flesh jiggled before arriving at a rippling halt.

Tiger could smell the collusion in the room, and she neatly managed to get herself between Fat and Luther so that they could not see each other without shooting her dead in her tracks. She smiled *mucho simpático* at Fat. "Well, you're an old friend and…Luther doesn't have many old friends. And, seeing as how this place is so bare—say—maybe you can help us with our redecorating? Luther says you're a decorator." The honey dripped from her fibbing lips.

Luther had to smile. Tiger was onto him, and Fat was on his own. Fat would have to stew in his own juices, which were considerable.

"Oh, yes," Fat stewed, "I do decorating. Yes, I do that."

Tiger picked up on it quickly. "Or are you a wood carver? I forget."

Fat was in the fire and sputtering. "Oh, well. You might say I'm a…kind of a wood-carving decorator. I decorate with…carved wood."

Tiger moved on victoriously because the fat rat had been cornered by the relentless cat. "I see. Well, why don't you make yourself comfortable?" She became hospitably Biblical. "Take the east wing. You'll be warmed by the morning sun."

"Yeah. Thanks." Fat was pleased to be off the griddle, and he picked up his bags like a hungry bellhop. "My, ah, logs will be arriving soon. I'll carve you something nice.

Maybe a little table—or a fence." He lost himself in the next room, which was big enough, tripping over his bags in the getting there and arriving in the east wing like an elephant come to die.

Tiger stalked over to where Luther sat at his workbench, quietly humming "The Star-Spangled Banner." She was superbly in charge, waiting to see if Luther wouldn't be the first to fill the silence. He was. "Not much work for a wood carver these days. And he has a son in prep school, a little Italian kid. I believe his name's Pinocchio. Nice kid, but he lies a lot, has this big nose that keeps growing. Terrible." He said all that while never looking at her.

"And how long do you know him?" Tiger asked.

"Should I face the jury?"

"Just answer the question, please."

"Oh, I'd say I know him about…twelve minutes. But it feels longer." He knew she wasn't buying, so he got a little closer to the truth. "I know him from around. I mean, I pass him on the street and I say, 'Good morning,' if it's morning, and 'Gee, it's raining,' if it's raining. And yesterday I said to him, 'Hello, it's Wednesday, why don't you move in?' And he said, 'Good-bye, I'll see you Thursday,' and there he is, big as life." He glanced at Fat and added, "Bigger."

Tiger probed deeper. "Why did you lie to me?"

Luther became a prominent plastic surgeon. "It was necessary. I discussed it with Dr. Gillespie and the entire staff, and we all agreed to lie because we had no way of knowing if the operation would be successful. It could have left your face horribly scarred. Happily, it turned out well, and I'm pleased to inform you that you'll be playing the piano again in no time. Or is it the *kazoo* that you studied at Juilliard?"

Tiger was more upset than angry. She didn't want to broach the issue head on because that always ended up with her the loser. Still, if she let it go without some cursory questioning, it would be her own private Munich for sure. "Luther, have I been—Is it really so difficult being alone with me that you have to pick up…itinerant wood carvers?"

"Actually, I don't know *what* he is. I mean, I wouldn't count on that fence if I were you. Also, I'm not sure I like the fact that you're so suspicious. You do that a lot, you know. It's not a pleasant trait." Having thus turned the gun on *her*, he got up and wandered out of the apartment and into the hallway. He started down the four flights, never looking back to see if his pet Tiger was padding along behind, which she was.

She chose not to raise her voice at him because she knew she had too few options left. Still, she spoke to him in motion, her words seeming to arrive at his ears just as he was going on to the next landing. "If you didn't lie so often, I wouldn't have to be so suspicious."

"If you weren't so suspicious, I wouldn't have to lie so often. I could lie only occasionally, every now and then, like a normal man. But, no—with *you* around, I have to lie all day long."

"Which comes first—the chicken or the egg?"

"The rooster." He stopped and turned up at her, holding his arms open so that when she walked eight stairs down, she was wrapped within them. He hugged her as he stood there, just two steps closer to earth than she was. And he pressed his head against her chest while his big hands moved lower and kneaded her buttocks. "I love you," he said, as his hands moved on in search of greater treasure.

Standing above him as she was, he seemed a painfully small boy with an Oedipus thing for mommy's ass. She smiled down at him, allowing his hands to go further beneath her skirt because it was so evil, so unlike anything she'd ever done before she met him. She really couldn't believe what he was doing with his big fingers, and all of it without as much as a by-your-leave. The cad, he was tugging the elasticity from her panties as well as the starch from her argument. Incongruity. Unpredictability. They were his most fabulous weapons. He could make her hurt for him in the most outrageous situations. And once having transported her into such delightful euphorias, he could get her to forget everything and agree to anything.

He looked up at her from between her breasts, resorting to a moment of undeniable sincerity, which she immediately recognized as his way out. "Tiger, I don't know. I don't know why some months have only twenty-eight days. Or why, when a person gets a bop on the head, he gets a bump instead of a dent. Or why I asked Fat to move in. I mean, he's not terribly attractive. And I never really thought he'd show up. But he's here, so let's let him hang around a couple, two, three, four days—till he finds another place. And then—out he goes. Okay? Is that okay, baby?"

She was dissolving in his hands, no longer really caring to argue the topic under discussion. For who would she be fooling? Oh, why, she thought, why did women have to give themselves away so quickly? Why the instantaneous lubrication at just a touch? How many arguments over how many centuries had ladies lost because a male finger found access? She kissed the top of his lying head and melted upon his studious digits. "Okay," she said. "It's okay."

"Good. Then it's settled." He quickly collected his tunneling fingers, and she felt as though her insides had gone along with them. He went hustling down the remainder of the stairs while she stood there in painful dilation, the petals of the rose crying mutely for the return of the bee. Then she followed him down, knowing full well that any time he chose, he could use his shamelessness as a battering ram against her twenty years of uptight morality. It was a measure of their relationship. He could make love to her on the roof of a church, in full view of the congregation, any time he wanted and twice on Sunday. And when he had concluded the debauchery, he could get her to sing the lead in the next hymn.

When she reached the street, he was already fifty yards away but was running back toward her, looking as though he were about to shout, "Look, Ma—no cavities!" Instead, he swept her up in his winged arms, and beaming like a happy fool, he said, "I need you. We can make it work. We really can. This town *needs* a dentist, Arlene. You've seen the cavities. Well, the mayor and the City Council have offered us that little house on Elm Street—rent-free! It'll be a great place for the kids. Stay with me, Arlene. Stay."

Tiger was at once the Three Graces—Helpless, Hopeless, and Hapless. "Does it have a sycamore tree?"

"A big one. A hundred feet high and twenty around. Rover will go out of his fucking mind."

"A garage?"

"Enormous."

"A white fence?"

"With ivy."

"I'll stay."

He lifted her up and whirled her around as in a perfume commercial. Why was it that it never seemed real to her? He kissed her and said, "Can anyone feel about you as *I* do? Name six."

She smiled at his nuttiness. "Jesus…"

"Good. Five *more* and you win a seat alongside the guest of honor at the Last Lunch."

"Luther…"

He had already broken away and was taking, two at a time, the stone steps of a nearby brownstone. At the front door he turned and motioned for her to hurry and join him there. Still riding the tail of his momentum, she climbed the red steps, and together, they entered the building's vestibule.

There were confronted by a directory listing the building's tenants. There were a dozen names, each with a bell button before it. Luther grabbed her and spun her around as in Pin the Tail on the Donkey. "Close your eyes and stick out a finger." She complied, naughtily extending her middle finger. "Not *that* one," he chided. So she retracted the obscene digit and shot out, in its place, the traditional index finger. "Good," he said. "Now—*go!*"

He nudged her toward the directory, and blindly her finger pressed a random bell button. Up there somewhere she could hear the caustic buzzer ring. She opened her eyes and leaned back against Luther and waited for God to strike them both dead. Instead, a grating female voice floated down the stairwell. "Exterminator?"

The door had been opened, and Luther shouted up at it. "Yeah!"

"It's about time!"

"Yeah!" He checked the name on the directory: Brewsterman, 3B. Then he grabbed Tiger's hand and led her up the stairs, saying nothing. It was a way of life.

Mrs. Brewsterman stood in the opened doorway, a sour lady, fiftyish and belligerent and fair game. There was a kerchief over her hair, but it didn't really cover the big pink curlers that stuck out like the lethal points of so many land mines. Tiger felt that should the woman get nasty, they could touch her points and explode her. And wouldn't *that* curl Mrs. Brewsterman's hair?...

Mrs. Brewsterman was not happy. Her gnarled hands lay tapping her thick hips, and her voice shot out like a top sergeant's. "You certainly take your sweet time. I called eight thirty this morning."

Luther was at his best, a lying fool with the conviction of Christ. "Sorry, but seems like the whole city's crawling with mugwumps." He flicked something from his shoulder, making a face and watching it fall, then stepping on it, and grinding it into the floor. Tiger did likewise with whatever thing was on *her* shoulder. All she ever needed was the first line of any of Luther's songs and she could join right in. Just to sweeten the illusion, she reached across at Mrs. Brewsterman and flicked at something on *her* shoulder. But she never had a chance to grind it into the floor because, somehow, it flew away and Tiger watched it go.

Mrs. Brewsterman recoiled in revulsion. "Mugwumps?"

Luther was leaning offhandedly in the doorway. "I'm afraid they're all over." He feigned a sudden confusion. "You *did* call about the night-crawling mugwumps, didn't you?"

"I called about ants...Night-crawling *what?*"

Luther explained patiently and professionally. "We've

had eight calls in this building alone, but most of them are from the first floor. Mugwumps start at ground level, you know."

"I didn't know."

"Anyway, you're on the third floor, and since it'll take 'em awhile to work their way up, we'll come back later—when *they* do." And he actually started to leave, smiling reassuringly at her as if to establish his nonreliance on the hard sell.

Mrs. Brewsterman grabbed at his sleeve, and he jumped, pretending that he thought he'd been attacked by an entire gaggle of mugwumps. "What about the *ants?*" she asked, growing increasingly concerned.

Luther made light of it, even laughing. "Listen, once the mugwumps move in, you'll wish you had the ants back. Anyway"—he started to leave again—"keep all your soap out of the way. Most people keep it in the refrigerator. Only don't get it mixed up with your cheese, a-ha-ha."

"Soap?"

"Do you use it?"

She didn't quite know how to take that. "Well, we *bathe*."

"Yes. That's where the trouble starts." Luther had her and he moved in for the kill. "Soap is a mugwump favorite, Mrs. Brewsterman. Anyway, don't worry about it for now. You'll know they're around when you see the little black shells in the soap. They leave their pincers there, you know. And—oh—keep your toothpaste tubes closed real tight. They love to burrow in there, especially if it's a fluoride. They love fluoride. I guess it's good for their tiny little needle-sharp teeth."

There was a pause, and Tiger, sensing that she was

on, filled the void. "Do you use Crest, Gleam, MacLean's, Pepsodent, Colgate, Plus-White—"

Mrs. Brewsterman was unnerved. "Not *all* of them, but—"

Luther asked, *"One* of them?"

"Well—yes."

Tiger delivered it like a death sentence. "Oh."

And Mrs. Brewsterman protested the verdict. "What do you mean—'oh'?"

Luther swept in from the right flank. "Do you have any children?"

"Yes. Yes, I do, but—"

Tiger came in from the left. "Their beds are at least thirty-six inches off the floor, I presume."

"I don't know. I never measured."

Luther repeated. "You never measured." He made it sound like "How can you be so stupid?"

Mrs. Brewsterman's arm reached out and hooked Luther's. "You're doing my apartment *now.*"

He resisted. "There are others who called first."

"Now!"

"It may not be a problem yet—unless they're breeding."

She practically pulled him into the apartment. "Right now!"

Luther allowed himself to be coerced into Apartment 3B even though it had not been properly scheduled for service. "It's eight dollars and thirty-three cents, plus tax, per room. But you'll save twice that much on soap and toothpaste in no time. Also, you won't have to throw away your provolone cheese like so many people do. Also, Mrs. Brewsterman, let's hear no more about ants, okay? Ants are *nothing* next to mugwumps. Ants don't kill."

Tiger followed Luther into 3B, where, at the kitchen sink, they whipped up a concoction of baking soda, Ajax, Mazola, and Pepto-Bismol. They boiled it till it foamed, then diluted it and applied it, and Mrs. Brewsterman was never again bothered by night-crawling mugwumps.

9

Fat Chance was very much on their premises. He kept pretty much to himself, setting up house in the east wing and rarely venturing west. Tiger wasn't exactly delighted with his presence. She could see, from time to time, the odd sidelong glances he aimed at Luther, who innocently (or diplomatically) never seemed to notice. Fat busied himself with a lot of intense paper work—graphs and notes and calculations. He had a whole collection of little index cards that he'd read to himself fairly regularly, after which he'd roll on the floor laughing.

Fat had refrigerator privileges which seemed to Tiger like giving Jumbo carte blanche at a bacchanal. But she kept her thoughts to herself, never once bringing up Fat as a topic of conversation with Luther. How long Fat would stay— she'd have to leave that up to Luther. But at the rate Fat was attacking their food supply, he figured to be dead of the gout within a week. And Tiger visualized his bloated corpse, swelling up in the living room, pushing the furniture against the walls and the lamps out the windows. He'd be too big to move, and the Health Department would have to come in and explode him as they'd do with *any* beached whale. And then they'd—

Luther took the shoe box from the closet. Tiger hated that. Really hated it.

The dirty old alley was well off the beaten path, in spite of the fact that it was right smack in the middle of the island of Manhattan. It was about fifty yards long, and it separated the sides of two old buildings by no more than fifteen feet. Even at high noon the sun could never find a way to shine in, and as a result, the alley was like a scene out of Hogarth, dank and grimy and foreboding. Its grubby inhabitants were primarily rats, cats, and overflowing garbage cans. But on occasion, one might see there a pretty girl shining shoes.

The man sat on the empty orange crate, looking down between his legs at Tiger as she worked over his clunky brogans. He looked at her long hair and lithe body and at the way her small hands stroked the brushes with sex-laden authority. He liked her hands, liked the thought of them and what they might shortly be doing to him. He smiled at the body curled up in front of him, on her knees, head down in so servile a position. Shortly he would be a king.

No one else was in the alley, nor was anyone likely to show up. It was a once-in-a-lifetime thing. And it had all been instigated by *her*, the girl between his legs. Never in his life had he been able to pick up a girl. Yet there he was, at the age of forty-four, in an alley with a beautiful young thing, and it had been at *her* suggestion.

He watched the shine come up on his shoes until they looked like headlights. He knew it was getting to be time. His trousers were growing tight, and his asthma was beginning to kick up and, if there was a God in heaven, it had all better happen soon. He reached down to touch the hair of the beautiful girl.

Tiger gave the two shoes a few quick slaps of the buffer, and like a drummer finishing up, she even made the rag crack. Then she got to her feet and stepped back from the leering man and said, "There you are, sir."

He was uncertain. "Pardon?"

"There you are"—she smiled like a bright elf—"your shine." And she gave each shoe another quick smack of the cloth, just for fabulous good measure.

"Is that it?" he asked, his dreams taking flight, his trousers growing looser.

"Yes, *sir*. All done."

"Just a...shoeshine?"

"Oh, *no*, sir. Not just a shoeshine, but the *best* shine these shoes have had in many a day." She began swiftly to close up shop, putting away the polish and brushes and things and moving with a practiced haste because she could already hear his hot breathing. "Okay, sir," she said to reiterate, "that's it." She tapped his shoes the way real bootblacks do when indicating that the shine is over.

"Hey, what is this?"

"It's two dollars, thank you." And she smiled at him with angelic innocence.

"Yeah, I know, but—say?"

She reminded him, "I *did* tell you two dollars."

"Yeah, but—for two dollars, I thought—"

"Well, I don't know *what* you thought, sir, but you were obviously under an erroneous impression." The trick, of course, was to allow no discussion. She slapped the little shoe box closed and, almost rudely, nudged the orange crate with her shoe, a clear indication that it was time for him to get off.

The man got off the crate, but the incident was not yet concluded. He had not come forty-four years to be conned. "Yeah? Well, when a cute piece of tail motions me into an alley and says, 'Two bucks for a shoe job,' well, I got a perfect right to think—Say, what kind of farmer do you think you're dealing with?"

He moved toward her, more out of annoyance than lust. And she found herself backing up against the cold brick wall. "Now, sir—"

He wasn't one for rape because he was a businessman and a solid and reasonable citizen. So he placed both of his hands against the wall, one to either side of her head, and he offered her a deal. "Look, kid—you want it to be *five* bucks? Okay, I've got five bucks. You want ten? Okay, ten. I'll pay. I'm not cheap. But I want what I pay for. I want a nice little...shoe job. Understand?" He eased himself closer to her, the bulge in his trousers arriving before the rest of him. He couldn't believe he was involved in such a scene but, damn it, the kid had him so excited—he was going to get *something* from her, *anything*. Even if it was just to put himself in her lovely young hands, he was going to get *something*. He began to unzip his trousers. It was incredible that he was doing it—and what would his wife say?—but he was doing it.

Tiger tried to make herself more concave than she was, but she was pressed against the brick wall and it wouldn't give. The man's breath was of onions and Binaca, and it mingled with the vivid aroma of Right Guard in combat. She saw his hand and what it was doing. She had some options. She could scream. Or she could kick. Or she could kick and scream simultaneously and then run. She hated whenever it was cut this close. She felt sorry for the man, really. But she'd kick him anyway. And she was about to when she heard the whistling coming toward her—"The Star-Spangled Banner."

The tall man came sauntering up the alley, his hands jammed into his pockets, loose and easy. "Hah thayuh," he called buoyantly, deep into some kind of Alabamian accent. And he smiled as he came up to Tiger, as if he were the original country bumpkin. "Am ah next? It's two dollahs, raht? Ah heayah it's the bayest shan in town." He looked down at the man's shiny shoes. "Woo-eee, will yo all lookit that! That thayuh is some shan! Why, ah can actually see maself in them thar shoes. Ain't that the nuts?" He waved down at his two reflections. "Hah thayuh. Yoo-hoo. Hah thayuh, Jasper. Watcha all doin' in Noo Yawk, boy?"

Thus reinforced, Tiger stuck out an upturned palm to the man and smiled sympathetically at him but said it all the same. "Two dollars, please."

"Yeah?" The man wasn't sure of anything. Except that, after forty-four years on earth, he couldn't just leave with his tail between his legs, especially since something else was then occupying that part of his anatomy. He zipped up his trousers.

Luther went into his idiot smile. "Ah have to sayuh, suh, that that shan is wuth it. Ah ain't nevah *seen* such a luster.

Two dollahs? Heck. It's a steeyal."

The man had pretty much figured it all out even before Luther opened his mouth. He sized up Luther and convinced himself that it was his forty-four years of age, not his lionlike bravery, that should be taken into consideration. He dug out his wallet and grumbled. "When this city cleans up you hippy-bippies, it'll be a better place. Goddamn anti-American dope fiends." He peeled out two singles, glad that he had them because he knew if he forked over a fiver, they'd thank him for the tip. "Two dollars for a shoe job! Well, it'll catch up to you, believe me!"

Tiger was pleasant, but she couldn't resist it. The man was, after all, a dirty old man, and he hadn't taken out his thing just to *air* it. "For *three* dollars you can get a *boot* job."

The man started away up the long alley, choosing to leave in the opposite way from which Luther had arrived. "I'm coming back with a cop, you no-good, goddamn, flag-burning beatniks. And you two better not be here when I get back, goddammit." He walked a little stiffly, but he walked straight. It certainly was an accomplishment.

Luther and Tiger watched "Joe Smith, American," make a right turn and disappear at the end of the alley. "See that?" said Luther. "Typical middle-class American sex fiend. Has to read something sexual into everything. It's shameful, just shameful."

Tiger was upset and a little sick to her stomach. She usually *was* after each aborted shoe job. But this time she was more upset than usual, and she made no attempt to hide it. "Luther? Do we *have* to do this?" She had shoe polish smudges on her face and looked like Judy Garland playing an urchin.

"Do *what?*"

"This. Do we have to do *this?*"

"Yes."

"Why? We don't need the money. So why?"

"I don't know."

"Luther, every time I do this shoe job bit, I feel like a hooker."

He picked up the orange crate and led Tiger out of the alley. "You're too harsh on yourself."

"Luther, please! I said I feel like a *hooker!*"

"You're being silly. Hookers don't shine shoes. They're too busy *removing* them."

She stopped walking. "Just the same, I hate it. I really do. One day it's going to backfire, and I'm going to end up getting raped. Raped, Luther! And for only two dollars!"

"And you'll be worth every penny of it, I'll tell the world."

"And I hate this god-awful alley. It smells of piss and beer." The tears were coming. "And I don't like it anymore. It holds no romance for me anymore. I don't want to *come* here anymore."

"Funny you should mention that. I was thinking of staking out a new place, a nicer neighborhood. A place where everybody's got black shoes so you only need one polish. And where, when you take their money and turn them down, they keep their mouths shut and go away in peace. It's a fine place, really."

"Where is it?"

"Would you believe the Rectory behind St. Patrick's?"

It was a desperate time for Tiger. She wasn't getting through to him, nor would she, nor could she. So she just said, "Yes."

"Shall we say—Sunday, after mass?"

"Yes."

"Shall we go home now?"

"Yes."

10

Fat Chance was in the east wing, working diligently at his thing, shuffling papers, making notes, and on occasion laughing out loud at his little index cards. Luther and Tiger sat on the floor, their backs against the wall, at the far end of the west wing, but where they could see Fat and discuss him openly without his hearing them.

"Luther?"

"Yes."

"Why does he laugh like that?"

"Fat people are jolly. They're also light on their feet. Wait'll you see him dance. Have you ever seen him dance?"

"No."

"It's a laugh."

"What do you suppose is on those little cards?"

"I don't know. Funny dance routines."

"Now he's writing again. What do you suppose he's writing?"

"I'm kind of hoping it's his will. Wait'll you hear him

cough. Have you ever heard him cough?"

"He's been writing like that for two days."

"Maybe he's writing a book."

"On little cards?"

"Why not? Lincoln wrote the Gettysburg Address on a paper bag."

"Think he's writing a book?"

"Yes. A book of funny dance routines, as told to Arthur Murray by Peg Leg Bates."

"I hope you're wrong."

"Why?"

"Because he's only got two more days to finish it." She turned to him and shored up her point. "Luther, you distinctly said he'd be out in a couple, two, three, four days. You distinctly said—"

"I know. But I like having him here because he gives the apartment ballast. Ever notice how *this* side of the pad always used to sag? Well, by keeping him in the east wing, it somehow seems to even the whole thing out. Have you noticed how things don't tip over as much as they used to?"

"You said four days."

"What if he's writing a Russian novel? I'm sure no one interrupted Dostoevski. Would *you* have interrupted Dostoevski? Tolstoi maybe—but not Dostoevski. Nabokov and Pasternak perhaps—but not Dostoevski. Nobody ever interrupted Dostoevski. Not even Lincoln asking to borrow a paper bag."

She stood up, miffed. "For all our sakes, I hope he's sending out postcards telling people of his new address— in Mozambique."

"Where you going?"

"For a walk, okay?"

"Okay. But don't pick up any strangers."

Tiger went walking. Down the steep stairwell to the street. Into the neighborhood. Just a stroll, nothing more intended. Just a pleasant meandering during which she inhaled much of the air that New York still had left. She had noticed of late how stuffy the apartment had become, and for no reason she could attribute it to. Unless it had something to do with Fat's invasion of her territory. That was probably the answer. No matter—it was good just to get away and get her head back on straight.

People passed by in all directions. Some in pairs, some in groups. Most smiling, jabbering, happy. And it seemed to her that she was the only one traveling alone, single-o, sans stud. Worse, that feeling of "minus man" was beginning to smack of permanence. The once-soft wax was hardening, the clay setting, ossifying, petrifying. She walked alone and knew that something had to be done if anything was to become of her life. She considered alternatives, but for some reason, all that came out was some passing reliance on the defunct French Foreign Legion.

Then the sound dropped out, as though her hearing had fallen into a hole, and she was aware of only her heartbeat. And that was none too regular, only loud. It was disquieting, that absence of sound, a reflection of her own void. She knew that it would only be temporary because it had happened to her before, always just following some verbal altercation with Luther in which she found it impossible to get through to him. It was internal pressure that brought it on, the keeping of things inside, and it was relieved only by a short separation from him, a small walk in which she indulged

in serious deep breathing, long, drawn-in inhalations...
slow, extended exhalations. That would do it. Her hearing
would crack back into place; only it would seem louder than
before, and much more acute. Cars. Doors. Heels. Voices.
Laughter. All came at her in monumental detail. And this
time was no exception. Her volume turned up as suddenly
as it had previously turned off. And with the volume came a
clarity of focus, an exaggeration of audio minutiae that was
superhuman and unsettling.

Young men and women were suddenly screaming love
things to one another. Things meant to be private, but Tiger
could hear them all, every syllable.

Or was she reading lips? But if that were the case, then
where was the music coming from? Loud, cacophonous,
dissonant. Stravinsky versus Bacharach, two falls out of
three. Mozart versus the Electric Armpit, fifteen rounds to
a decision. How could a person lip-read music? Who sings
Braille? Who listens to skywriting? Who was the sweet kid
last seen entering the alley with a shoeshine box under her
arm? Who was the slender puss in the big boots too tall,
coming up well over her knees? Where were her clothes?
What was that ominous overtone, that bizarre foreshortening
causing the darkness to squeeze in? Who was responsible for
the filthy alley? Whatever happened to Fun City? Explain,
please, why no one else is around. No one and no thing in
no place at no time. Why the crumpled dollars in the little
clenched fist? How many—three? The price of a good boot
job, no?

The pimpled, unpleasant, leering man—why? Leaning
against the brick wall and mostly in shadows—how come?
Unbuttoning his trousers and taking a few barefoot steps

toward her, tromping on her eardrums. Ten yards to go. Nine, eight, seven. Music up. Rachmaninoff. Percussion buries screaming. Darkness masks horror. Paper covers rock. Man mauls Tiger.

At the other end of the alley, aha! The U.S. Cavalry. "The Star-Spangled Banner" in a contrapuntal whistling. Another figure emanating, loose and angular, and familiar. Nine, eight, seven...

She let herself plop against the wall and slide to a sitting position, where she waited for whichever man got there first. The big palm cupped her face, tilting it up at his. "Baby?"

It takes a time for a fog to clear, certainly the better part of a seaside morning. It takes awhile to mark the separation between nightmare and death wishing, between topsy and turvy. A kiss on the cheek turns the lights back on. Safe at home. Spoons up, darling. Hi, there.

Luther looked down at her tiny bare feet. "Hey, nutsy, where're your shoes?"

She tucked her head within the hollow of his shoulder, very glad to be there and how do you do. "They went away."

"Yes. Shoes will do that from time to time. Come on, baby." He led her out of the alley. "I had a pair of shoes once—they went away, too. Didn't leave a note or anything. Just went away. I've never allowed myself to become attached to a pair of shoes again. Who needs that kind of heartache?"

They were well out of the alley, but Luther could still see how shaken his little barefoot girl was. So he just walked with his arm about her, heading her home, knowing that it was no time to press her with questions. He had rescued the kitty from the tree. It was unimportant how the kitty had gotten there.

Tiger gradually came out of it and wanted to talk. "Luther, I think—I mean, I think I *imagined* that…I was about to give a man a boot job."

"Cash or credit?"

She looked into her small fist to see if she still had the three crumpled dollars. She hadn't. "Credit."

"We'll put it in Accounts Receivable. Did you get his name?"

"No."

"Shoe size?"

"No."

"Could somebody at Forsheim's identify him?"

"I don't know."

"Hmmmm. Looks like a case for Louie Nizer."

"Luther?"

"Hmmmmm?"

"Do you think I'm getting…sick?"

He had his opening. "Actually—I think you're gonna get sicker."

She pulled up short. "Explain, please."

"Well, you know how two times out of nine I don't lie."

"Yes."

"Well, this is one of those two times. What I tell you now is gospel. Cross my heart and stick my nose in a buffalo turd."

"Go on."

He suddenly became honest and tender. "I do bad things to you, I'm sorry. I know I'm unpredictable and irresponsible and—I know I'm disrespectful and that I'm *this* way, then *that*, and that I have difficulty in telling the truth, and that I keep you always under pressure—" He stopped and then

81

became his old flip self again. "Well, Tiger, my sweet, my heart and my dearest, there's going to be a little more weight in the east wing." Before she could say anything, he decided that it wasn't quite the time to take her home. So he hooked her arm and walked her off into another direction. "Come on. Let's get something to eat."

She padded alongside him, barefoot and frightened, into the sangria place, where they soon sat opposite each other at a little table in the back that featured a candle stuck into an empty wine bottle. The wax had dripped over the lip of the bottle and deposited ten minutes' worth of paraffin on the wooden table before Luther wiped the remains of his sausage sandwich from his mouth and cleared his throat for attention. "Now then, where was I?"

"You were zigging. You had just zagged, so you were zigging."

"Ah, yes. Now—" He was big and attractive and at his best. She knew it and he knew it. "Though I admit that inviting Fat to live with us *was* an unconscious expression of my insecurity at being alone with you—"

"When did you admit that?"

"Just now."

"True." She had tried, feebly, to offer some resistance to his verbal juggernaut, but it had been such an obvious ploy that all it did was weaken her position. She knew it, and he knew it.

"Where was I?" he asked, confident and formidable.

"You were zagging."

"Correct. Yes. Though I own up to the fact that inviting Fat to live with us was an unconscious admission of my insecurity at being alone with you—"

"Prologue, all prologue."

"The fact that Leon Darvac has just this night, while you were out, moved *in*—*that* is not of my doing."

She repeated the name without expression. "Leon Darvac."

"Yes. That's his name. At least that's who Fat *introduced* him as. I suppose he *could* have another name, except he *looks* like a Leon Darvac. He really does. And that pleases me because I never, in my whole life, met anyone who looked even *remotely* like a Leon Darvac."

It was never said more sweetly. "You son of a bitch."

Luther fell all over himself with abject, introspective sincerity. "I swear to you, God strike me dead, if he can find the time, Fat says that Leon called and said his building had been condemned, primarily because it was falling over and—"

She placed her hands palm down down on the table in an expression of "let's stop the shit." And she said, "Question?"

Like a schoolteacher, he pointed to her as though she were a mile away in a large auditorium. "Yes. The young lady over there. Speak up, please."

"We have no phone. When Leon called, how did Fat answer?"

"In a very loud voice." She had him, so he smiled and allowed her the point. "Actually, that's a very good question."

"Yes, isn't it?"

He leaned across and touched her hands, his long arms neatly straddling the candle, causing the light to play up at his face so that he appeared as a smiling spook. "Tiger, before you get all crazy—"

She slid her hands out from under his. "Keep your

hands off me, Black Bart. I may be a simple schoolmarm, but I can shoot your eyes out with the derringer concealed within my ample bosom."

He played it her way. *Anything* to avoid the head-on confrontation that was gathering steam. "You have a derringer in there?"

"Two of them."

"Loaded?"

"Cocked."

"Son of a bitch."

"Bastard."

He tried again, pulling back from the candle because his nose was just this side of catching fire. "It's all true, darling. Leon's building actually began to collapse. At first they thought it was the Mad Bomber of London."

"Ah, the Mad Bomber. At it again, is he?"

"Well, he *has* been blowing up half of London. Why, just a fortnight ago—"

She swung her head away and looked elsewhere. "Waiter?"

Luther spoke hurriedly. "Anyway, Leon grabbed whatever clothes he could and came right over, lickety-split. But he won't be staying long because Fat's been working on this idea which Leon says can't fail. I think it has to do with his dancing index cards and—well—that's it." He sat back and rested his case because he had no other choice. "That is definitely it."

Rebuttal. "Well, it's not *quite* it, is it?"

"Pardon?"

"I mean, somewhere along the line you gave it your okay, no?"

He twitched defensively. "Well, I gave it...tacit approval.

Understanding the circumstances, I couldn't quite bring myself to say no."

"Did you nod? Did you give it a shrug and say you'd talk it over with *me?* Did you shake a little? Did your nostrils dilate?"

"I'd like to call my lawyer."

"Did you flex the muscles in your manly jaw?"

"I furrowed my brow."

"Oh, *that's* good."

"Yes. I thought so, too." He demonstrated his furrowed brow. It looked like an aerial view of a recently plowed Kansas hayfield. "How do you like it?"

"And Fat interpreted that as approval?"

"Yes. A common mistake, don't you think? After all, a furrowed brow means different things to different people."

"Would you like to know what it means to *me?*"

"No. Only to Fat. It was his furrow. To properly judge the furrow, you'd have had to have been there when the furrowing took place. I will not have my furrows analyzed out of context."

"Listen. I approve, okay? I approve of *everyone* moving in." She got to her feet, her toes flexing on the dirty floor. Then she blew out the candle in a move that was dramatic and total and final. And she looked down at his wondering eyes and delivered her decision. "I also approve of *me* moving out."

She walked away barefoot, breaking stride only once to jig on a hot cigarette butt. Luther sat for a moment, the curling smoke of the expiring candle causing his eyes to tear, and he was genuinely moved because he thought he was crying and he hadn't cried in so many years that, obviously, she was very, very important to him. He left a Monopoly card on the table instead of money. It read: "Take a Ride on the Reading." Then he scooped up the tip that was left on a nearby table and caught up with her outside, following her huddled figure as she scurried for a bus that had pulled up from out of nowhere. He got on the bus right behind her, almost losing one foot in the closing door. Gallantly dropping his freshly pilfered tip into the coin box, he bowed to her and said, "Allow me."

She looked at the bus driver, a disinterested sort because it was late at night and he was pooped. "Driver," she said, "this man is bothering me."

The driver never looked up, just tossed the words at Luther from over his shoulder. "Don't bother her." Then he stepped on the accelerator and Tiger went caroming down the aisle like a partially deflated medicine ball, plopping into a seat and leaving no room for Luther.

Luther was still up front. It was his turn to make a report to the driver. "Driver, that girl has no shoes on."

"Put your shoes on." The driver never spoke again, probably for the remainder of his life.

Luther navigated the aisle better than Tiger, choosing to hang onto a strap a few rows diagonally behind her, even though there were three dozen seats available. There were a handful of passengers, just a smattering of half-asleep people going God knows where. Luther spoke loudly, not caring who heard. "There is no way for you to move out, Clarissa. I'm locking you to the radiator. If you haven't given your word by wintertime that you won't try to escape, you'll fry when the steam comes up."

Tiger kept looking out the window, determined not

to hear, rubbing her toes together to ward off frostbite. The random questions of her own mind popped like hot corn kernels. Who was she? What was she doing fleeing that madman? How far could the bus take her? Dubuque? Des Moines? What was her name? Janice. Yes. Whatever happened to Janice? Does anyone remember Janice? You there, going into the drugstore—remember Janice? And you, sir, peeing in the doorway, remember little Janice?

Luther was straphanging back there, but maybe if she blinked her eyes thrice, he'd disappear in a puff of green smoke. She heard his voice and knew that he was striving to be serious in spite of his delivery. "I happen to be mad, okay? I have no doubt about it. My brain is already pledged to Harvard and my pecker to Radcliffe. I also have no doubt, Loretta, that you are my only hope that my testes will not end up on somebody's plate at the Racquet Club." He finished up by prodding a drunk. "It's a curse, I tell you. I'm cursed with being in love with a graduate of Jones College."

Tiger wheeled angrily in her seat, frightening half to death the lady in the seat directly behind her. "You creep! Not a graduate! A *dropout!* And not Jones! Smith!" Then she turned forward again, conscious only that the woman behind her had gotten up and judiciously changed her seat.

Luther let go of the strap and made his way up the aisle, sliding into the warm and vacant seat behind Tiger, where she'd know he was sitting though she'd be unable to see him. He picked up a *Daily News* that had been read by eight people already. "Ah," he said, contemplating the newspaper, "fifty-seven degrees in San Francisco today. What a goddamn accomplishment for the city by the Bay." Then he leaned forward and whispered into her ear. "Tiger,

I give you my oath. Fat and Leon can stay for only as long as it takes them to get their idiot idea off the ground. I swear. I oath. What the hell do I care about San Francisco? San Francisco means *nothing* to me."

Tiger got up and changed her seat, depositing herself in one farther toward the front of the bus. Luther did likewise, once again ending up directly behind her. He soon leaned forward confidentially again. "Don't turn around, don't act startled. Pretend nothing unusual is happening, but your ass is on fire."

Tiger moved to change her seat again, but Luther moved first and faster, sliding quickly alongside her, pinning her where she sat with the bulk of his big body. He grabbed her hand. "And if they can't do it in a reasonable amount of time, out they go. Do you read me, babe? Tiger? I'm oathing. You cannot ignore a man who is oathing."

She could. She could keep looking out the window, which she did. A seedy-looking man across the aisle, a decent sort, hardly heroic, felt obliged to intercede on Tiger's behalf. He tapped Luther's arm. "Maybe she don't feel good."

Luther barked at the man. "You a priest?"

"No."

"Then don't dispense religious dogma with such craven alacrity or you'll find yourself excommunicated on a good Samaritan charge, you humbug and charlatan."

"Oh." The man sat back and wished he was a plainclothesman with the power to arrest and kill simultaneously.

Luther stood up in the aisle and became an Indian. He looked dourly down at Tiger. "Tall Chicken make his pledge. He take full-um responsibility. Our tepee will once again belong to just Tall Chicken and his squaw, Horny Hen. All others will be gone before too many moons have passed. This-um no bullshit."

Tiger tried not to laugh. She tried hard, but a snicker escaped. It was all so absurd. She was sitting on a bus the destination of which she had not the slightest idea. She was sitting there barefoot while a Scarsdale Indian was propositioning her. She looked up at the tall redskin who stood frozen with his chin thrust out like an ad for Mussolini, and she said, "And how long is a moon, Tall Chicken?" And she knew full well that her question had signaled total capitulation to his lunacy.

"How the fuck should *I* know?" And he pulled her from the seat and yanked her up the aisle, screaming to the driver, "Getting off, please. Getting off. Please cease the fucking bus, sir."

The bus rambled over to the nearest bus stop, and a moment later, the two dispossessed Indians were standing nowhere, on a corner they knew nothing about, with nothing going on around them other than a few lampposts. Luther pressed her hard against him and spoke down at her though she wouldn't look up. "Dammit, Tiger, when have you known me to give so much ground ever? So you come on back and trust me. That's what it's all about, isn't it?"

Her face came up, featuring a wan smile. "Oh, Christ..."

Luther checked his wristwatch and looked up the street for another bus like the one they had just gotten off and knew nothing about. "Where the hell is that bus? And they have the nerve to raise the fares. It's a good thing I never pay. I'd be pretty damned pissed-off." Tiger watched as he launched delightfully into a new and wonderful snit. "This city"—he was shouting—"the dirt! The filth! The garbage! The vermin running around! Where the hell is a cop? You can never find a cop when you need one in this goddamn city! Never!" He cupped his hands and hollered through them. "Cop! Cop! Hey, cop! My kingdom for a cop! Why can't I find a cop? A *fag! I* can find a *fag* when I want one, but not a cop! How come not a cop?" He turned minty. "Yoo-hoo, oh, coppy? Arrest me, coppy, I'm a molester. Run me in with your big stick, you old wonderful cop! Oh, coppy!"

The night closed in around them, but somehow they got home. Tiger never quite remembered how. Perhaps Luther picked her up and flew her home. Yes, that seemed logical.

11

Because her little bare feet were so sore, Luther carried Tiger piggyback up the stairs. He opened the door to the apartment, and she slid from his back. The first thing they saw, leaning against the wall like an evil cypress just oozing swamp, was Leon Darvac. Wickedness was all over him. It exuded from his enlarged pores and rippled in his pink and watery eyes. Even in his powder blue cardigan he was a singularly unattractive creature, and Tiger immediately spelled his name backwards to see if it carried any significance. "Noël Cavrad." Nothing. Unless it was the Swedish diminutive of Noël Coward, but that wasn't likely because there was no way in which Leon Darvac could have claimed to have been of Scandinavian extraction. He had a rodent-like head, with flat, pointy ears and no chin to speak of, and had he been standing there munching on cheese, she'd have climbed back aboard Luther's back and, resorting to the whip if necessary, been well on her way to somewhere west of the Mississippi and east of Rangoon.

Introductions were made, and Leon, to his credit, withheld offering his leper's paw. Whatever his malevolent malady, he somehow respected the fact that it was contagious and abhorrent and fatal, and he didn't choose to pass it along to the masses. He also had about him, unfortunately, the smell of a spoiling corpse in a tight sauna. The poor man obviously suffered from athlete's foot, for which there was no known cure and no known cologne to mask its presence.

Tiger found some old sandals for her scuffed feet and sat quietly beside Luther, for Fat was holding court and deference had to be paid. Fat had his papers and his little index cards spread in organized mounds all over the table, and he seemed solidly sure of the case he was about to present to the academy. The only truly discordant note about him was that he no longer seemed the plain and pleasant tubby fellow of old. Rather, he was displaying another shade of his personality. It was the sudden air of the con man, the elan of the practiced hustler, the liquid shiftiness of the accomplished conniver.

"Here's the bit," Fat said. "I've worked it all out very carefully, and Leon, who has the mind of a computer, concurs. The idea is simple, precise, feasible—yet bold. We, all of us, charge a monthly membership fee. And we have a central telephone number." He turned officiously toward Luther. "We'll need a phone. Make a note."

Luther obediently found a piece of paper and a pencil. "So noted," he said. And Tiger knew that a small explosion was silently building, for Luther was not a man to fall in line so quickly behind *any* authority, let alone a fat one who didn't pay rent.

Fat smiled appreciatively at his vassal, accepting his

servility, then proceeded. "At any time of the day or night, a member can call in and"—he took a puff on a suspicious-looking cigarette, squeezing out a lot of drama, and then completed his point—"and we will tell him a dirty joke."

Tiger felt her toes curl involuntarily, but Luther merely made another note on his paper. "Any time of day or night…a dirty joke. Got it."

Fat went on. "We call it Dial-a-Dirty. I've already got a collection of about fifty of the raunchiest jokes of all time." He held up his pile of index cards as evidence. "Nuns, animals, fags, dykes, ducks, goats, you name it."

Luther asked innocently, "Horses?"

"Three," said Fat, very pleased with himself. "Numbers eight, twenty-two, and thirty-seven."

Luther scribbled down the numbers. "Eight, twenty-two, thirty-seven. Check."

Fat sailed on. "Believe me, and Leon concurs, there's a fortune out there in the land of over forty. And, shit—wouldn't they just love being at one of their cocktail soirees and dialing Dial-a-Dirty and then becoming the hit of the whole fucking evening?"

"Fish?" asked Luther.

Fat replied, but with a dash of annoyance. "Whales, sharks, squids…and two electric eels."

Luther scribbled it all down. "…and two electric eels."

Fat kept going. "Now, when a member calls, he gives us his name and number and we charge his account twenty-five cents. Then, at the end of the month, we send him a statement. It'll work. Leon concurs."

Luther looked up like an interested student. "How do we line up members?"

Fat was pleased at the intelligent question. "Easy. We print up cards and pass 'em out on Park Avenue and Madison Avenue and the like. Those jerks, they'll cream just to have a new dirty joke to tell in their office. What the hell *else* do they have to brighten their days?"

Luther still projected vital fascination, but Tiger could perceive the obtuse angles of his Lutherian sarcasm. "Fat," he said, "it's wild, just wild. And as long as we have a phone, we can make a couple obscene calls on the side, right? Why, there's a couple ladies in this very building that—"

"I think we should try to keep the line open, Luther." Fat had taken it so seriously that Tiger came close to wetting her pants. Fat explained his reasons. "You see, we have to proceed on the assumption that the phone'll always be busy."

Luther kind of sulked. "Not even *one* call to Two-E? It'd make her day. She's a cross-eyed spinster with no tits. I don't see why we can't put a little fun in her life."

"Sorry, Luther. It's a luxury we just can't afford."

"I see," said Luther, nodding his understanding, "and Leon concurs?"

"Leon concurs."

"Can Leon concur for himself?" asked Luther as he looked over at Leon, who nodded his concurrence to Luther's satisfaction. But Tiger could feel Luther stiffen alongside her. It would be just a few moments more—

"So you see, Luther," said Fat, "the idea is pretty God damned workable. Matter of fact, there's absolutely nothing wrong with it."

"Well," said Luther, warming to the issue at hand, "the *first* thing wrong with it is the phone will not be in this apartment."

Fat was very CIA. "No one has to know. It's going to be an unlisted number."

"Swell. But what if the Community Chest calls? Unlisted numbers have never stopped the Community Chest or the Salvation Army, for that matter. And how about Billy Graham?"

Fat wasn't sure of anything. "What *about* Billy Graham?"

"What if he calls? What do we do, tell him the one about the nun and the cow and the Boy Scout? And surely you realize that, at any moment, I can get a call from the UJA. What do I do, tell 'em the one about Golda Meir and King Hussein's camel?"

Tiger was dying inside, but nothing on the outside gave her away. She just sat immobile, her bright eyes unblinking as Luther pointed to her.

"Now Tiger here, though there's no way you could have known it, is forty-two and a half percent Negro. So what happens if someone from the NAACP calls and wants to speak to her, and *you*, in your innocence, you tell 'em the joke about Eldridge Cleaver and Snow White and the Three Honkies? We'll have the Black Panthers on our asses in no time."

Tiger faked a sneeze. It was *that* or die.

But Fat maintained immaculate equilibrium. "Luther, members will have to identify themselves."

"I see. No blacks, eh? Well, I want no part of a segregated filth club."

There was a slight rise to Fat's delivery. "Luther, they can be black. They can be *plaid*, with *sequins*, with *Coca-Cola* comin' out of their assholes—it doesn't *matter!*"

"It would matter to *me*. Coca-Cola?"

"Luther"—Fat was striving for control—"all we do is match their names against their membership numbers. In that way we never get into any trouble over the phone."

"There's *another* way not to get in trouble over the phone—no phone."

Fat's confidence was wobbling along with the rest of him. "I've figured it all out. It won't *work* without a phone."

"How about if we stick Leon on the roof with a pair of dirty semaphore flags?"

"Luther—no! We need a *phone!*" Fat was becoming frantic.

So Luther became calm. "How about...obscene chain letters? You fuck the girl whose name appears on the top of the list and, within a week, seven airline stewardesses are flown to your house where they blow you till you're three foot six."

Tiger got up and looked out the window, knowing that it had all better end soon. Fat kept nodding, "No...no ...no..."

So Luther ended the discussion. "No phone."

Fat looked up, undaunted, even reborn. "Well, I was afraid you might take that attitude so—" He shuffled about some papers and came up with a new batch. "I have an alternate idea. We teach dancing at people's homes. All the latest stuff. Leon's a master at it. Anyway, the gig is, though it *looks* like we're teaching dancing, what we're *actually* doing is booking orgies and—" He stopped abruptly and lapsed into pitiful apologia. "We'll need a phone. I'm sorry."

Luther stood up, signaling *finis*. "Well, I tell you, Fat—you better figure out a way to make it work with carrier pigeons, 'cause Poppa don't allow no dancin' in here." He became very threatening. "Now the pair of you pornographical wizards, get your bodies back into the east wing before *all* of us tip over onto Sixty-first Street. The Housing Authority concurs."

Fat and Leon shunted off into the east wing, taking their papers and shutting the door behind them. Luther went over to where Tiger was standing at the window. He stood behind her, wrapping, then locking his arms about her waist. "Don't worry, puss. It's not going to happen. If I can't make obscene phone calls on my own phone, it's just not gonna happen." He squeezed up closer. "Hey, puss-puss. Ever hear the one about the lunatic and the tiger? Well, it goes something like this." And his hands groped upward and slid over her breasts and searched for the buttons on her blouse.

She pulled away. "I'm sleepy."

And she went to sleep alone. And Luther respected that.

12

The Art Boutique was a very posh, very expensive place. Its denizens that night wore furs, flaunted blank checks, and dropped names. The women, even the short ones, walked tall and strode with confident libidos. The men held back and felt rich because they were. No junk in that place, nothing middle-class or low-brow. Tiger, dressed as nicely as she was, still felt out of her element. But Luther, in tux, was once again in his Jack Bergman period, and he moved in and out of the cocktail sippers with pompous assurance.

On sale that night, owing to the auspiciousness of the occasion, were Grecian statuettes, carved miniatures, the proceeds of which were to go toward the establishment of some kind of worthy endeavor like the laying of the cornerstone for the School for the Stammering Blind.

Tiger held the finely tooled sculpture that depicted Cupid and Psyche in classic embrace. It was of white marble, delicate and breathtaking, with an attention to detail not found in carvings rendered after A.D. 500.

Luther came alongside her, swishing his maraschino cherry dizzy in its manhattan glass, while stuffing his face with hors d'oeuvres that kept coming by on silver trays with offers to "take one, please." He had contended with Tiger's concentrated silence practically all day long, and now, with the liquor warming both his belly and his temper, he chose to tolerate Tiger's mood no longer. "Might as well say what's on your mind, Inspector. It's this devilish waiting that I cannot stand."

"Some things don't have to be said," she said, saying nothing and proving her point.

"Oh, listen to her," said Luther. And some passing fool did just that, actually stopping and listening because he had overheard Luther's directive. Upon discovering that there was nothing forthcoming from Tiger, he then moved on, dribbling his champagne on a crotchety dowager, who gave him the good talking-to he had been seeking since his Oyster Bay mother had stopped spanking him ten years prior.

Luther spoke directly into Tiger's ear, softly but with resolve. "I'll tell you the truth, cat—I may be sick, but I ain't *that* sick."

"That's very encouraging." She strode away, still holding the statuette up before her, admiring its beauty.

Luther tagged after her. "I'm sick, but not for the reason *you* think."

That stopped her. "Oh?"

"Yeah. Oh. So Fat is weird. Big deal. We all know nothing's gonna come of his ideas. He just likes to talk because he knows he's never gonna get it all together. So why the hell are you so uptight about him?"

"I am *not* uptight about Fat."

"No. Of course not. You *always* walk around like there's a steel pool cue up your poop."

"Phrasemaker."

"Ramrod."

"It's not *Fat* who bothers me, okay? It's *Leon*. Super Rodent."

"So he's a little shady, so what?"

"Shady?" She had to laugh. "He's so shady that anyone within five feet of him loses his suntan. He's so shady that whenever he walks across a lawn, grass dies."

Luther stepped back and flicked a smile of admiration at her. "Very good, darling, I must say."

Tiger barreled on. "He's been with us a week, eating all our cheese, and I've yet to hear him say one word."

"Did it ever occur to you that he might be a deaf-mute?"

"And did it ever occur to *you* that both he and Fat were supposed to be gone in a few days and that if they stay any longer, they become ours by common law?"

"I've always wanted children."

"Shouldn't they be born of woman?"

"I don't know. That's a very messy procedure."

Tiger held the statuette up to a man who she correctly assumed was in charge. "How much is this, please?"

He smiled authoritatively. "Three hundred eighty-five."

"Pounds?"

"Dollars."

"Thank you."

"You're welcome." The man walked away, wondering why he couldn't quite place that girl who was so obviously of the international set. Perhaps he should have quoted the price in marks and francs as well. And escudos. And rubles.

Luther bellied up to Tiger and let her have it squarely. "We haven't balled since Fat showed up. And I tell you, I have to get rid of this poison."

She applauded him sarcastically. "Oh, bravo. Well struck. Lord Byron could not have stated desire more poetically."

"Fuck Lord Byron."

"Browning, too, I suppose."

"Browning, Shelley, Keats, Joe Namath—the whole bunch of 'em!"

She turned away. "You're shouting."

He followed her. "Fuck shouting." He grabbed her arm and stopped her. "What the hell *are* you—on *strike?* Just because I'm trying to help a couple lost cats make their way?"

She faced him. "I don't like them around. I'm sorry, but aren't *we* trying to make our way, too?"

"Right."

"So? Why are we keeping them around when the landlord distinctly said 'no pets'?"

"At least they don't *steal*, like *we* do."

"*You* steal. I *don't*."

"You qualify as an accessory and a moll."

She grabbed his lapels and pulled him roughly to a corner. And she held him like that, crudely, shaking him as she spoke. Her grip on him was firm, but her words came out all soft. Again, her own dichotomy. She wanted to kill him and kiss him simultaneously. "Luther, when it was just you and me, it was fine. That was nice. We had our problems, but we were all right. Now, suddenly, there's *four* of us. How did that happen?"

"Amoebic fission."

She ignored his observation and kept pressing her point

which happened to be a good one. "I love making love with you—but not in a crowd. Not in Yankee Stadium. I'm terrified that when you roll off me, sixty thousand fans will cheer because you scored."

"Nobody spills over. That's the house rule, and they know it."

"And it's a fine rule as far as it goes. But one of those two is shooting something so weird that he's…flying around every night. I thought we drew the line on just pot." She began to feel the frustration gathering in her throat, so she quickly walked out of the gallery and stood on the street, where she swallowed air in big drafts.

A few moments later Luther came moseying out. He tapped her shoulder confidentially and turned Mexican. "Hello, lady—care for to see hot postcards? Very feelthy."

She walked away, but he stayed right on her heels. "You weel like thees. Very clear. Also, beeg show in cantina at two o'clock, si? Speedy Gonzales going to fuck two girls from Vassar, and on the ceiling. Come one, come all."

She stopped walking and faced him angrily. "You say you want me to stay. Yet you keep melting into a self-induced crowd. At which point all this rebellion goes foggy on me. And I forget what it is I'm rebelling against. I mean, *sir*… until I met *you*…*I* was the Establishment." Her phrases came out in tearful lumps. "I want to stay with you, Luther. But you have to give me a climate I can thrive in. I'll cross over to anywhere with you, but you have to help me. You have to…Jesus, Luther…take my hand."

He took her hand. "Gotcha." And he pulled her close. "I love you. Tiger, I love you. And I want you to have something that's really worthy of you. Something…

beautiful." He opened his jacket, and she saw it there. The statuette. She gasped in disbelief, but he spoke first. "And now I think we should be running along."

And run they did. Luther like a disinterested miler, just chugging along, pacing himself. Tiger like a refugee, continually looking over her shoulder at whatever must surely come chasing after. Ultimately she found herself laughing as she ran. It was all so preposterous. And soon, laughing or not, they found themselves caught right smack in the middle of Park Avenue traffic. Luther protected her from the zooming cars, choosing to hold her close with one arm while directing traffic with the other. He also shouted at the rushing vehicles. "Too much lead in your gasoline there, Al!...Polluter! Polluter!...Get a horse!"

She was laughing so hard that he practically had to carry her up the stairs. And she was very glad to be laughing because it dissipated some of the pressure. She felt that she had made her point without being forced to leave. She felt good and fine and hopeful. In the west wing they studied the statuette of Cupid and Psyche. Then they tried the same position. Then they did some variations on the theme. Then, at about 3 a.m., they thawed out a frozen pizza and ate most of it. At 4 a.m. they got back into bed and burped until 4:30, at which time they fell asleep in Position No. 94, visions of anchovies dancing in their heads. Starting at 7:30 a.m. and well on into the rest of the following day, they were on a diet of Rolaids and Alka-Seltzer. It rained hard that afternoon, so they never really got out of bed. They just lay there, on their backs, watching Cupid and Psyche carry on their three thousandth year of almost motionless copulation. Those Greeks, they had a way.

13

Tiger climbed the stairs, having to stop at every landing to rebalance the heavy bag of groceries she had bought at the all-night grocery. She thought of leaving it right inside the hallway door, going up without it, and sending Luther down for it. But of late, Luther had been so incredibly amorous that it would be at least an hour before he'd let her go, and if the bag hadn't been stolen by then, certainly all the frozen foods within would have been disastrously defrosted. So she carried the bag up by herself and wondered happily if she'd ever get a chance to put it down—or would she be holding it all the while Luther took his pleasure? The compromise, of course, would be to set the bag down just prior to entering the pad. But that would take some of the danger out of her life. So, no—she'd carry it in, devil take the hindmost.

She knew she must have sounded like Frankenstein's monster, clomping up the stairs with so deliberate and ponderous a tread. So she wasn't surprised to see the apartment door swing open. It would be Luther doing

Dracula, and he'd flash his eyes and exclaim, "Walcum to my kethil." She wasn't quite right because it was Leon, and he wasn't saying anything. But then he never did. The question *then* was: what was *Leon* doing opening the door? From the look on his squeezed and narrow face there had to be something very, very wrong inside the pad.

"Where's Luther?" she asked, not waiting for an answer, moving right past Leon, hearing him shut the door behind her—and lock it. That door had never been locked before. Through plague, drought, and famine it had always remained open. The click went off in her mind like a grenade. Lock the door against *what?*

She stood still and looked toward the east wing because that's where it was happening. And then she walked slowly toward it, Leon following on little rat feet.

Luther was leaning over Fat, who was lying on some cushions, totally freaked out and sweating like a horse while smelling like an ox. Luther kept caressing Fat's face with a damp washcloth, hoping feebly to bring him around, but making no progress whatsoever. Fat was out of it, off somewhere, riding a bummer and muttering incoherently about earth and sky and fire and ice. And Tiger could only guess at what dark things fluttered about in his damp head.

Luther looked up and saw her. He got to his feet and handed the cloth to Leon, indicating with a nod that Leon was to take the next shift. Leon concurred.

Luther took Tiger aside. She was still holding tightly to the big bag of groceries, as if it were a part of her, her baby. She looked into Luther's face, waiting for an explanation while fearing the worst. Luther tried to take the bag from her arms but couldn't. "What is it?" she asked.

Luther was icy. He pointed to the west wing. "Go inside."

"Luther—what?"

He was very short with her. "Shut up. Get inside…He overdosed."

"On what?"

"I don't know. Lavoris." He yanked the bag from her arms and set it down on a table.

She spoke with an uncharacteristic lack of emotion. He had put her through so many hoops that she no longer had any emotion available for purposes of display. She was totally uninvolved with the words that came out of her. "What do we do?"

"We wait."

"You don't really know what to do, do you?"

"If you like, we can pray." There was a bite to his answer, a strong hint for her to back off.

"Shouldn't we call a doctor?"

"Yes. About three years ago." Again, his answer came out dripping with acid. Gone was his usual levity. And Tiger could see the signal flag go up the hoist: "Don't bug me."

She watched as he turned his back on her and went back to Fat. He took the cloth from Leon, and kneeling alongside Fat, he attended the pudgy fellow with an unmistakable tenderness. "Come on, Fat. Come on, fella."

She came over and stood above him. "You're good with busted things." He said nothing. She took another moment and reintroduced the question because logic was demanding it. "Shouldn't we call a doctor?"

He never looked up. "A doctor'll put him in jail…Will you shut up!"

The cruel pragmatism of his reaction meant that he

wasn't to be questioned further on the matter. So she walked to the farthest corner of the west wing and sat down in an almost fetal position, but in a spot where she could observe all the action if she chose to look.

Luther's voice was a light-year away. "Come on home, Fat. Come on in." He was patting Fat's face with his big cushion of a hand. "Fun is fun, Fat—so come on in. Luther to Fat, Luther to Fat. Come in, Fat, Over."

But Fat showed not the smallest inclination of coming in for a landing. He was up there alone, flying blind, his instrument panel wigwagging, little bulbs flicking on and off, bells gonging, buzzers sounding. Tiger knew that he was perilously close to death. That Fat might die was a dreadful enough thought. Yet somehow Tiger could accept that. Because dying is where everyone is headed. Living is what gets them there, but dying is the eventual and unalterable destination. Also, isn't there a solace to dying? To most people, doesn't dying mean conclusion to agony, finale to travail, novocain on the half shell? Wasn't the *real* anguish, if one is of a sensitive nature, reserved for the *survivors* of any particular dying? After all, there has to be a general tidying up, a lid tacked to the box, a hymn, some assuaging chants, a good-bye, a couple of tears, and a few shovelfuls of dirt. In *this* case, however, there'd be something else. Police.

Luther would be arrested, of course. And she along with him. Unless an invisible derrick could sneak in and cart Fat's zeppelin remains across that last river without anyone's getting wind of it. Bail would be required. Not for Leon. Leon would be shot trying to escape. But bail would be a possibility for Luther and Tiger because, really, your honor, we're not bad kids, just misunderstood and unhappy. But

who will put up my bail? said the Little Red Hen. Hi, Dad—
it's Janice. Yes, I'm calling from New York City. Yeah, the
Big Apple. Listen, Dad? Can you send some money—I'm
in a bit of a jam. Oh, fifty thousand dollars should do. But
you'll get it back, Daddy, I swear, every quid of it.

> Do you ken John Peel with his coat so gay,
> Do you ken John Peel at the break of day…

It was the high school choir again, mostly girls, sounding
a lot better than they had in that god-forsaken auditorium.
Practice makes perfect, girls. Keep up the good work, girls.
Oh, pooh on you, Miss Nenner with the laughing baton.

The statuette of Cupid and Psyche stood on a nearby
table, looking quite like a religious talisman that had been
placed there to lend meaning to Fat's passing. The night was
dragging on, a gimpy snail with miles to go, miles to go.
Tick-tock, oy-vey. Withdrawal. Introspection. Recollection
and trauma. And once again, Tiger was up to her pretty ass
in a goulash of time and events.

MOTHER: "Janice, this is very serious. Very. I don't
know what's on your mind. If you can't handle intermediate
algebra, how do you expect to go *on* in life?"

Only small movements in the east wing. Luther and Fat.
Leon bringing new and cooler cloths. When will the fever
break? Tear up your petticoats, ladies, and we'll use them as
bandages. And get the children back to the wagons? Ready
whenever *you* are, C.B. Action. Sound.

CHORUS: (Miss Nenner, bless her, conducting):

> Oh, Shenandoah, I long to hear you.
> Away, you rolling river,
> Oh, Shenandoah, I long to hear you.

Away I'm bound to go
'Cross the wide Missouri.

BRIAN: "Baby, sooner, or later, we have to. That's why I got the station wagon. Janice? Jesus Christ, Janice—what the hell you doing? Jesus Christ, Janice—that's my hockey stick!" Huffing, puffing. Womanhood. Yay!

MOTHER: "You what? You lost your what? With who? Brian who? Janice, do you realize I'm your *mother!*"

Passage of time. A clearing up of the skin. Yay, Clearasil. Dullness. Predictability. Conformity. A parlor car to college. Here's your beanie, here's your room; here's your bucket, here's your broom. Study. Be something. Don't disappoint. Write often. Straitjackets and tethers. Careful thought. A decision.

DADDY (long distance): "It wasn't easy to send you to Smith. We made sacrifices, Janice. We denied ourselves. And now you tell us you're dropping out? Well, let me tell you— Janice? Janice!...Operator? Operator!"

"Tiger? Tiger?" Luther.

Tiger moved her face, and the early sun was on it, ending the morass, silencing the pitifully small voices of an insignificant but demiheroic life.

Cupid and Psyche cast a long shadow across the floor. It ended on Luther, who was standing above her, pushing out that immense and thoroughly irresistible smile. "It's okay. Fat's okay. But we lost the baby."

She didn't laugh. It was work enough to get her heart going.

"Come on, Tiger. Fat made it."

She was out of control of herself, totally. And she found

herself getting up without having to rely on his extended hamhock. "I *didn't.*"

He gave her a funny look. "What?"

She was resolute. She had crossed over. She didn't want it anymore. She was preparing her closing comments. "You're all fine. You've got your...thing. *I'm* the fish out of water."

"Stay calm. Cool, baby."

"I'm calm. I'm cool, baby. I just don't belong." She went about the gathering of her things. Her valise with the Smith sticker yawned open, ready to travel. Her clothes fairly flew, of their own power, into the valise. The wounded ballet dancer, she'd take that, too. In it went. "Luther, I am so tired of all my false exits..."

"Don't be silly."

"I have to go."

"Don't be silly!" The second time he said it he shouted it. Then he subsided and laughed at himself for his outburst. "Tiger. Hey, peace. I'm sorry. I'm upset. This...hasn't been a picnic." His arms were around her, sweeping her in. "I'm very tired."

"I'm sorry for that. But I'm not your moll or your accomplice anymore. I'm your...ex." He'd had it coming to him for so long. And she had to state it boldly if she was to believe it *herself*. Her belongings were about as packed as they'd ever be. She had difficulty closing her oafish bag, and Luther wasn't about to help, so she sat on it until it gave up and rigor mortis set in. It whumped closed, and she snapped the lock to keep it that way. Locks were snapping all about her that night—that morning. She felt as though she were in an old news photograph as she picked up the valise— "Refugees fleeing Pnompenh before Cong onslaught. UP

Wire Photo."

Luther spoke with an odd control that was just one note short of rage. "I promise—they'll both be out of here by morning."

She faced him, trying to get through to him, once and for all, and for final. "Luther, *they're* not the issue. *I* am."

"No. Don't be silly."

She felt a thumping internal pressure. She was having trouble breathing again. He was doing it to her again—refusing to see or listen. Her lungs were wheezing inside her like a tired old bellows. "Luther, please—I don't want to panic, but I can't breathe in here. I'm all right outside, but I can't breathe in here." She picked up her bag again and made for the door. Movement helped her bellows pump. But it was like pushing a dying fish through water, forcing the current through its open mouth so that, perhaps, it could last a bit longer.

He stood in her way, but not as a barrier. His arms were spread helplessly. He was so futile she could cry. "Tiger—I love you."

She stood in front of him, feeling as though she were a kid running away from home. She wanted to stay but she had committed herself. "You bring me down, Luther. You really do. And the deeper I go, the harder it is for me to breathe. It's a warning. You're going to kill me. I have to go. Gee. I'm sorry—" She turned sideways, the better to squeeze past him, and he didn't stop her. She went down the stairs as well as she could. But it was an accordion in her chest, no longer just a bellows. An accordion filled with milk and featuring a slow leak. She didn't look back. She didn't dare. She just dragged her valise hammeringly against the stairs and the guardrails. Some of her clothing was pushing out as if it didn't want to go. But she'd be damned if she'd let a chemise screw up her escape.

She heard him up there on the landing as she clambered down. "Where you gonna go?"

"Away."

"Where do I reach you?"

"You don't." She kept going. As fast as she could. His crazy voice following her down every step of the way.

"I'll get you for this! Nobody bugs out on me! Your days are numbered, Moose Garvey! You think you'll get away?"

She kept going. Going, going. Her valise battered again at the banister railings, a clumsy kid rattling a stick along a fence.

"The squeeze is on, fink!" His voice was big and frightening. "You won't be able to move without wondering if you're backing into a shiv!"

She kept thinking—never stop, never stop! He isn't my problem anymore, anymore!

"I'll hound you down, Moose! I'll get you for this! There'll be no place to hide! No door strong enough to keep me out!"

The bag kept knocking until it finally gave way, flying open and spewing its contents, twenty years of girl, every which way. But she was at the bottom, even as some of the pink things came wafting down at her. She gathered them like butterflies and stuffed them hastily back into the bag. Back, panties; back, stockings; on, sweaters; on, Vixen.

There were no more sounds from above. Nothing. But she was afraid to look. The air came hard to her. Her throat was a narrowing funnel. She had to get to the street.

The thick object blurred past her, missing her head by what—a foot? It landed with an elephantine whump and broke immediately in half, separating Cupid from Psyche forever, except for his one hand upon her heart. That remained. Symbolism, symbolism.

She shut the valise as best she could, which meant that it really wasn't shut at all, just carried under one arm and held shut with the other. She slammed it hard against the vestibule door, utilizing it as a battering ram. The door blasted open and slammed back at her before she could pass beyond it. She recoiled hard against the doorframe, and her shoulder began to pang instantly. But it didn't stop her. She bounced back and was through the doorway in seconds.

She reached the street and ran, opening up the distance between herself and the building, half fearing that a large rubber band tied about her waist would shortly snap her all the way back, squash against Luther's chest.

She kept going, filling her lungs with air, making noises like a panting fox, but never looking back.

Behind her, so far back that he was out of sight in the creeping dawn, Luther stood on the top stone step of the building. He screamed into the murky ocher. "Yeah! Run, Moose! Run, run, run! Keep running, Moose! And try to hide! Hide, Moose! Hide, hide, hide!"

She ran, the air clearer, her valise no longer filled with rocks. His voice receded. It was farther and farther away, screaming, back there, frightening and pitiful and unreal. "Tiger! Tiger! Tiger!"

She ran. It was very late. No one on the street. No one to see and attest that this episode in her life had ever really happened. Just that voice, a primal caterwauling, trailing her far longer than it should have. "Tiger..."

Run, Janice, run. See the dopey girl run.

14

The Marshal House YWCA accepted Tiger, even at that irreverent early morning hour. They gave her Room 1224. 1224, she thought. Christmas Eve. It must have meant something. She would have preferred 1123, her birthday. But if you can't have your own, Christ's ain't bad.

Anyway, there she was, back with the Establishment. The YWCA. Wild. It was the first place that had occurred to her. Maybe because it had a pool. But more nearly because, from her earliest days, it meant haven. Her room was basic puritan. Unemotional furniture, framed prints of the flowers of six Eastern states, and the smell of a dentist's waiting room.

It all had had an instantaneous soothing effect on her. Familiarity calming the soul. Recognition reducing the apprehension. And it was suddenly as though the years between her father's house and the Marshal House YWCA had never happened. She had merely stepped, remarkably, from her own little bedroom with the white curtains into another just like it. And in the process she had obliterated Smith, and Luther, and pot, and pain.

She went immediately to sleep on clean percale. No nightmare, no dragon. Only once did she awaken, and that because the names of the Seven Dwarfs had come to her in a flash. "Humpty, Blitzen, Agamemnon, Greed, Lust, Avarice, and Costello." She woke up laughing after perhaps but two hours' sleep. Yet it had been a caressingly beautiful sleep. She stretched and yawned, and marched straightaway into a shower that actually worked. Water, the temperature of which you could truly regulate. No more the big swing from solid scald to frigid freeze if the tenant upstairs flushed the john or ran a glass of water.

She sang, even washed her hair, and considered going home. She did that only because she knew that she had that option and that she owed it to her parents to give it at least one little thought. Which she did, and then dismissed.

She wrapped herself in a big white towel and sang "Born Free." Before meeting Luther, she had been a reasonably modest girl, an only child painfully inexperienced in what went on outside of Daddy's domain. As "lovers" she had had: Brian Morgan (once). Paul Emhardt (twice, both awful). Richard Butler (once, and better forgotten). And Buzz Maples (six? no, seven). Therefore, prior to hooking up with Luther, she had had…four men (if you wanted to call them that) for a total of eleven times. Eleven times out, including a stumbling loss of virginity. Eleven times during which she had experienced a torrid half orgasm (thank you, Buzz Maples, and your magic finger). As a result of these trysts, she had, by her count, brought on three male orgasms (Buzz Maples again, bless him) and caused semi-impotence four times (Brian Morgan, one; Paul Emhardt, both times; and Richard Butler, one—but for all time). She had carried that little scorecard around in her head until she met Luther, at which time all previous records tumbled and new heights of ecstasy were scaled that were without number and beyond counting.

That she was thinking once again of the former assaults and invasions of her person convinced Tiger not only that her life as a sexual creation was not over, but that it had, by all that was reasonable, barely begun. Thanks to Luther, she could climax. Good. She'd be forever grateful to him for that, and not to Women's Lib. But Luther was passé, sperm over the dam, and new men lay ahead. Perhaps a baker's dozen of them were lining up for her years to come. Stouthearted men, erect, devout, and passionate. And somewhere among them was Captain Perfect, a man with minimal hang-ups and maximum charm. She would marry Captain Perfect and would be as faithful as possible under the circumstances, taking on only an occasional lover just to keep her loins in shape. One of these men would be a marvelous accident, Mister Hello. He'd say "hello." She'd say "hello." And they'd end up, without another word, in the Royal Suite of the St. Regis, making wild love within mahogany walls with sconces and purple drapes looking on. Then they'd both go back to their own worlds and never try to reach each other again. Except—maybe once, they'd bump into each other in Abercrombie & Fitch. But they'd both be with their children and would only smile like old friends and then pass in the night.

Another lover would be Stanley Stud, an overpoweringly rustic man, a farmer or a shipworker, with the phallus and energy of a Percheron. They'd meet at dirty motels and crummy hotels and bang away on squeaky beds until he'd pass out drunk and she'd sneak away, through the seedy lobby, a lady of darkest mystery to the scrawny desk clerk who'd watch her exit with open-mouthed awe and rampant desire. Stanley Stud would be to keep her depths of passion properly plumbed. She would keep his phone number and call him from time to time, in Kansas or Singapore. And they'd meet like that, like wild bulls a-humping and a-bumping. And years later, after Stanley had gone on to his reward, his son—Solid Sydney—would have found her phone number written on one of his father's athletic supporters, and he'd give her a call, and they'd meet, like every eighth Tuesday, and she'd bring her magnificently toned body to his walk-up flat, and she'd crack his back for him and make his tattoos curl. And he'd roll over, covered with beautiful perspiration, and he'd say, "Dad was right. You are the greatest ball of all." And he'd ask if she'd be interested in meeting a few of his friends who didn't really know what a real woman was. And she'd insist on seeing their photographs first. And those she liked she'd make appointments with, and she'd be as wanton as she chose because no one would know her true identity, and her sweet, dear husband, Captain Perfect, would never guess at her other life. And when it came for her to die, at the age of ninety-four, a few hundred unnamed men would come mysteriously to her funeral and toss roses upon her coffin. Woman—fantasy is thy name.

She dried and warmed in the big towel and completed her unpacking, which really wasn't much. She placed the wounded ballet dancer on the bureau, where it could smile at her. She'd keep it forever, of course. Her children would ask about it, and she'd make up fabulous stories about how it was an enchanted doll, given to her by a prince from a faraway land. Thank you, Luther, she thought. When it's all said and done and is years and years behind and over, I will think on you kindly, and I will smile.

She had asked the old lady at the desk if it could be arranged so that a *New York Times* could be placed at her door—and there it was. She scanned the first page, nothing good there, and went swiftly, as in a conditioned response, to the classified ad section. She would find a job that morning, damn it, and she'd be back on her own feet in the real world where there'd be new dawns and bright fresh surprises. She found a pencil in the ladylike desk and made professional circles on the newspaper page, notes and scrawls that had to do with job prospects but that looked more like football plays. There were a few compelling job prospects, jobs she could handle. She was anxious to get started and was pleased with her bushy-tailed attitude. She was demonstrating that old resilience, individuality, indomitability, and style. She had come through a tricky experience and already had it well behind her. Good show, Janice. Press on and what ho.

She selected, for that day, one of the few remaining straight outfits she had. A nice yellow jumper, pretty green blouse, and ye olde and trusty brown shoes. They all welcomed her and hugged her warmly. She hadn't lost an ounce since the last time she had worn them, or gained an inch, or changed a physical whit. She had, instead, amassed experience, shed a lover, and gathered maturity. Her mind was clicking, framing logical thoughts, dispensing rational conclusions. It was 8:30 A.M., a fine time to slide the ship into the water. The sun was shining, the day was unfolding like a morning flower, and the phone was ringing.

That the phone was ringing was disquieting, for no one knew that she was there. Of course, it could be the lady at the desk, checking to see if the *Times* had arrived. But Tiger knew that it wasn't. She let the phone ring for a while. And by the time she fitted the receiver and placed it to her ear her blood was running cold. "Hello?"

It came out like one long, wiggly strand of spaghetti, Luther's voice. "Tiger? It's me. You're my first call. Remember Big Sur? Well, he's with the phone company, until he gets enough unemployment credit, after which he'll get himself fired. Anyway, he just installed me, sort of a bootleg job. It's my first concession to the outside world— an honest-to-shit telephone. Tiger, I'm putting it all together for when you come back. In the meantime, my awareness of your sick reliance on religion told me that you'd end up at some YWCA somewhere. Thank God you're not in the pool because you know you don't swim well. Listen, whadya have on for today? Don't tell me. The yellow jumper-green blouse ensemble, right? You're into your autumn thing, you and the trees, I know, I know. I hope you're not planning on looking for a job, but I know you *are*. Yet with your inheritance, Elizabeth, there's no need for you to *ever* work, except maybe as a nurse in some national holocaust. A job? You must have taken leave of your senses. Probably have a fever. Don't get your quinine tablets mixed up with your birth control pills or you'll end up with a litter of mosquitoes that look like me. Anyway, I'll call you tonight. Just remember the antidiscrimination laws. If you're qualified for a job, they *have* to hire you. So *what* if you're a Communist lesbian, there's still a place for you. And please, Wanda, wash your feet in the chlorine when you come out of the pool or else you'll be arrested and charged with first-class athlete's foot. Good-bye, my love. Take care. Look lively. And beware the jabberwock." Click.

"Bye." Tiger placed the receiver back upon its cradle. Spook, she thought. Luther, you spook. You goddamn big son-of-a-bitching spook.

There was no way for me not to find her. I could pick up her spoor in Calcutta in August. If I was in a ring with a dozen sweaty sumo wrestlers, and she walked by three blocks away, I'd know it. I know her sweet smell. I know the way it conspires with perfume and autumn and how it rides the breeze like Diana in search of Apollo. So finding her was no great trick. Getting her back, *ah—that was something else. Instinctively, owing to my years as a jungle fighter, I knew that a direct frontal assault would immediately be repulsed. She'd be expecting that; she'd be ready for it. So I fashioned another approach that was more nearly like a fox hunt. It's the only way I can explain it to myself now. I had set her running, across a course vaguely confined to Manhattan Island. I then put myself on her trail. She had one night's head start in the forests of Gotham City and I had already picked up her trail. It would be, judging from that, no contest. I would let the lovely beastie run herself tired for a while, and then, before it got too deep into the mating season, I'd close in on her and nip her on the tail and roll her in the grass. The important thing, as any member of a proper hunt club will tell you, is to allow the brittle thing no rest, no breather, no pause to refresh. Let her go, let her run free, even wild, but never let her think she can stop looking over her shoulder. Never let her believe that out of sight is out of mind. Haunt her. Find a way into her nighttimes. Harass her with intruding flashes of yourself. Keep her emotionally dependent on you. Feed that addiction. Let her run scampering and unfettered, boundingly oblivious, until she finds herself in some raunchy chicken coop, screaming for a fix. Then, sirs, members of the club, you will have her. And not until then. Tally fucking ho.*

15

Tiger was on the subway again, this time as a passenger, and in the rush hour yet, a true baptism of fire. She stood shakily, her arm looped about a pole, studying the *New York Times*. She had never learned the proper way in which to read that publication on a subway car. As a result, she held it fully open, as if she were a giant butterfly resting for a moment but still quivering its delicate wings. And as a result of *that*, she was flapping newsprint on smaller butterflies within range.

Through it all, Tiger managed to jot down additional notes in the margins of the help wanted section. Notes that superseded earlier notes. Evaluations, comments, odds. It was a scientific approach that would have pleased Napier. She had narrowed down the calls she'd make to four companies, each of which seemed to be in desperate need of typists. And for the four she had fixed on a sequence. And foremost in that sequence was the legal firm of Harper, du Bois & Malloy, because it smacked of prestige and tradition and class. Harper, du Bois & Malloy. It had a rhythm. Harper, du Bois & Malloy. The rhythm could not have been improved on by stringing out the names in any other order. Malloy, Harper & du Bois—nothing. Malloy, Harper & du Bois—not likely. Du Bois, Malloy & Harper—no. Harper, Malloy & du Bois—bad, wrong. Du Bois, Malloise & Harpoon. No. Harpoon, Festoon & Spittoon. Maybe. Spittoon, Balloon & Buffoon. No. Buffoon, Baboon & Maroon. Bumpkin, Lumpkin & Pumpkin. Piffle, Diffle & Whiffle. Muffle, Scuffle & Shuffle. Lexington, Avenue & Out.

It was a busy street, kinetic. Morning on Madison Avenue. Mad Avenue. Crazy. It was where it was at, the scene. Groovy. Still, it seemed brightly foreign. A sunlit nightmare. The structures, the pace, the noise—they all snapped at her heels, very unfriendlylike. She checked the address of a lofty skyscraper against that on her tattered remnant of a newspaper page. They matched. She turned to go in and was scooped up by a revolving door that then spit her out into a marble-floored lobby, the kind you slip on and bust your ass on when it's raining. She moved with the clicking group and was swallowed by an elevator. She stood in its whale belly with the rest of the plankton, being digested and regurgitated simultaneously. Two female minnows were discussing things, not caring or not knowing that all the world could overhear. Flotsam (in curlers) and Jetsam (in kerchief).

"Well, he didn't call again last night, but I expected that."

"He's playing it cute. Him with his new semi-executive status."

"Anyway, my hair is set for eight o'clock tonight, just in case. *Semper Paratus*, shall we say?"

"Mine, too. I'm streaked."

"I noticed. How much?"

"Thirty. Mr. Horatio."

"Thirty? Jesus."

"But it's Mr. Horatio."

"For thirty you should get Liberace."

"What can I tell you? I do the best I can. It's time for Arnold to call. Remember him from the last time?"

"Who could forget Arnold?"

"Anyway, if he calls—so be it."

"Listen, I'm thinking of wearing my blue dress with the mother of pearl buttons."

"Good. It sets you off nice. Your face."

"Of course, I'll have to stay at my desk all day, on top of the phone."

"Yeah."

"But he won't call at the office."

"He won't?"

"Nah."

"Why?"

"Come on, you know why."

"No. Why?"

"I'll tell you. But it's so evil."

The whale burped, and Flotsam and Jetsam blew out along with some other debris, and right in the middle of their story. Tiger would never know the ending. She smiled. It was a scene she had played before, only better. With sicker premeditation and greater flair.

The Harper, du Bois & Malloy interviewer was a female, efficient and phonily warm, camped behind a desk that had been conceived for the President of the United States. The name card on her desk, pseudo walnut, identified her as Miss E. C. Walker. Tiger loved that and, in her mind, immediately changed it to E. C. Rider in honor of Dennis Hopper and all the boys in the motor pool. Tiger loved the whole world of names she had stumbled into that morning. All these look-alike folks had names and initials to set them apart from one another. Fascinating. Like the faceless pro football players her father watched on Sundays. Big, lumpy look-alikes except for their names and numbers. Hats off to you, Aldous Huxley, you called it back in 1932.

E. C. Rider was going over the application blank that Tiger had filled out before being asked to wait along with four other look-alikes, Dora, Flora, Cora, and Clytemnestra. And now it was *her* turn before the bench. "Why did you leave Smith, Miss McAllister?"

Miss McAllister, Tiger thought. That was her. Janice Lynn McAllister. J. L. Mc. Daughter of B. M. Mc. Born in Ind., U.S.A. Where are you, Luther? I am sinking in a sea of alphabet soup.

"Miss McAllister?" The woman was looking at Tiger from over the rim of her bifocals. "Smith is a very fine school. Why did you leave?"

"Illness in the family." It seemed the thing to say.

"Whose?"

"Pardon?"

"Can you be more specific?"

"Yes."

"Well?"

"Well, it *is* a bit personal, but—" It all came flowing out, shades of Luther. "Both my parents contracted measles. It's very severe with adults, you know. I was called home from school because, at first, they thought it was scarlet fever, to which I was immune, having already had it. I've had every childhood disease there is, if it's of any use to you."

"It's not."

"In that case, they all pulled through." She smiled, shrugged, and decided to shut up.

"So you've never really worked at all, have you?"

Tiger could feel the job slipping away, unless she could come up with something more meaningful than measles. "Well, I didn't write it down because I didn't think you'd find it terribly relevant, but I *have* worked in the shoe business. Shoes and boots."

"I see." She was writing it *down! Gawd!* "At the retail level?"

"Well, I would say it was more...wholesale. We had...an outlet, but in one of your finer neighborhoods."

"I see. And was that a regular position?"

"No. It was kind of...off and on." Tiger was beginning to wish that she'd never brought it up. "We had kind of a very select clientele. Top businessmen, trend setters, community leaders. You know."

"Miss McAllister, have you ever worked at a *steady* job?" There was no doubt about it—the skids were being greased for Tiger's departure.

Which is why the answer came out of Tiger almost before she had had a chance to edit it. "Yes. In the exterminating field. Though it was pretty specialized. I mean, it was limited to bugs. We didn't deal with animals or crows or bunnies— just these bugs."

"I see. And just what was it that you did?"

"I killed them. I mean—not personally. I mean, I didn't

whomp 'em over the head. Nor was I even around when they died. I just sort of…set 'em up for the kill, if you know what I mean."

"No. Frankly, I don't. Just what is it that you *do* mean?" The woman was fast losing interest.

And Tiger knew it. So she quickly tried something else. "Well, no matter. Most of my efforts, because of my privileged upbringing, have been devoted to charities."

"Fund raising?" She seemed to like that. Fund raising connoted leisure time. Leisure time implied wealth. Wealth begets class. And class was what got respect, you bet your ass.

Tiger became lousy with class, even raising the tilt of her nose slightly. "Yes. I'm quite active in fund-raising endeavors. Worthy causes, you know. Have you heard of the UJA?"

E. C. Rider was suddenly not one for silly diversions. And she knew when her leg was being pulled (if only she could get a fella to do the pulling). "Miss McAllister, we need typists rather badly. Can you type?"

"I'm quite proficient at typing." A lie. In CAPS. Exclam. Close quotes.

The woman made some red crayon slashes on a card that you're not allowed to bend, spindle or mutilate, and then she thrust the card out at Tiger. "It's seventy-five dollars a week to start, provided you can do the job."

"Oh, I can do it." Heathen liar. For shame!

"Report to Miss Clarkson, in the steno pool."

"Her initials?"

"L. S."

"Thank you." And Tiger left, wondering why it was so bloody impossible for her to be serious about so serious a thing as earning a living. Part of the reason, and she knew it, was that she was not yet out of range of Luther and his big laughing. That would take more time. And until that time, she'd still feel him around, yakking away whenever she'd have to deal with the established world. Okay, she figured, sooner or later, she'll flick him off—like a mugwump. Meantime, she was walking down the corridor looking for the steno pool. And what the hell was the steno pool? Sounded like... psycho ward. She asked someone and wasn't surprised at the logical answer. Steno meant stenographer, of course. And pool was where the stenographers all hung out until someone came by and picked one of them out, like in a lobster pond. Miss L. S. Clarkson, a hundred and nine years old, grunted at Tiger's card and then tossed her, heartlessly, into the steno pool, where about twenty other orphan fish sat typing. It was disheartening and deafening because there were no windows, just overhanging fluorescent fixtures that looked like inverted ice trays. The girls looked as though they were attached to their typewriters via electrical umbilical cordicals. And all together they made a collective clackety-clack, whereas Tiger chipped in with an individual pippity-pip.

Anyway, Tiger soon had a pile of work before her, reports and things, that had to be deciphered, translated into legal English, and then typed neatly, in triplicate. And when *that* had been completed, she had to collate (staple) all the blooming copies. And after that, she figured, the foreman would come by, and if she had done it all to his satisfaction, he'd stuff a small fish into her mouth just as you'd do with *any* trained seal.

Tiger attacked her work studiously, secure in the knowledge that she'd never last the day and would shortly be out of the gloomy place and on the street again, looking for a less frightening and more satisfying manner in which to earn a proper living. Some of the things she typed up were more confusing *after* than they had been *before*. Obviously she had rediscovered her uncanny old touch of making a bad deal worse. It was a god-given talent that she hadn't resorted to since she screwed up the invitations to her sorority luncheon at Smith, causing half the guests to come a day early and the other half a day late. And here she was again, glue in the axle grease of civilization.

She had been at it for almost an hour when a nice but heavy-legged girl walked over from an adjacent typewriter. She looked over Tiger's shoulder and smiled at the page in Tiger's humming machine. "C-A-T, cat. Good."

Tiger shrugged good-naturedly. The jig was up. She'd be out of the pool, dried and dressed, and on the elevator in no time. Still, she figured, she'd put up a small struggle because to do otherwise would be shamefully weak. "I'm a little rusty. I'll pick up." Sure, she'd pick up. She'd pick up her day's wages and be gone.

"I've been clocking you," said the girl. "You're racing along at—oh—thirty words to the half hour."

"Yes, but they're big words." Tiger held up the last page she had typed. "Look. Scatological. Codicil. Supercilious... How do you spell 'supercilious'?"

"A lot better than *you* do. What's your name? Don't spell it—just say it."

"Janice McAllister." It sounded good. Very Scotch-Irish, fifth-generation Hoosier. Very American.

"I'm Martha Wesloski." She was a friendly type, perhaps five years older than Tiger, and apparently very conformist.

"First job as a typist?"

"I was with the Peace Corps in Africa. I did fifty words a minute—on drums." Was that her? No, damn it. It was Luther, using her mind, speaking through her mouth. Tiger attempted to rectify the quick lie. "No. That's not true." And she framed a sheepish smile. "I lie a lot. It's a habit I picked up. I'm trying to stop."

Martha glanced up at the big wall clock which supplied the heartbeat for the steno pool. It was nudging 10 A.M. "Come on. Coffee break."

"Really? But I've barely started."

"Come on. Our union fought the good fight for it. Don't ruin it for everyone."

Tiger got up from her typewriter, and it seemed glad to see her go. When it wasn't looking, she stuck her tongue out at it.

The white-jacketed counterman appeared in a square hole cut in the wall. Behind the hole was the commissary. The thing looked like an afterthought, as though the boss showed up one morning, saw the hole in the wall and said, "Let's stick a man in it and have him serve coffee." And the board of directors approved it ten to one, the one abstention being a doddering old spoilsport who never drank anything stronger than Chiclets. All about the counterman were coffeepots and chrome items that smoked and hissed and looked ice cold and very hot. A person could buy ice cream in that hole. And Cokes. And Drake's Cakes. Anything. The idea was for the people on Tiger's side of the hole to line up and, when their turns came, yell something through the hole and the man would scramble around as though he were shot in a shooting gallery. Then he'd pull himself together and hand the orders through the hole. It was a very effective way in which to utilize a hole in the wall, very purposeful and resourceful. The man worked swiftly, with a practiced speed, but under sweaty duress. He resembled all the countermen in all the drugstores in which Luther had hoisted tips. Nor was it beyond Luther to show up in that hole, just to bug her on her first day at work in the new world. He could do that, Luther could. And he might, too. And soon.

"Yeah? Next?" The counterman loomed up in front of her as a hands-on-hips torso. And he was very annoyed with the daydreaming girl. "Hey!"

Tiger delivered the perfunctory smile and addressed the man as though there were nothing odd about his standing there with no legs to speak of. "Coffee and a doughnut, please."

"How do you like it?"

"Oh, fine. It's my first day and already——"

"The *coffee!*"

"Oh. Black." She really didn't like it black, but she didn't want him to bother on her account.

The man poured the coffee. It steamed up in the wax cup like alligator bile. "Jesus," he said, nodding his head at the kooks he had to deal with.

"Yes." Tiger smiled, trying to carry it off with aristocratic grace, as the young Kate Hepburn would most certainly have done.

The cup of coffee and the glazed doughnut came through the hole in the wall as if fired in anger. Tiger ducked instinctively but soon realized that it had no fuse. She paid with a smile and thirty-five cents and followed Martha back to the steno pool, her new home, and there enjoyed her pasty repast. Somewhere around ten thirty all the girls went automatically back to work, so Tiger did likewise. Who was she to question how nature worked? She sensed that she was losing some of her individuality. Yet she realized that that was what she was being paid for. Life is give-and-take. Who said that? Robin Hood.

Pippety-pip developed into a slightly faster tatta-tat-tat. But in no way was it the classic clackety-clack of the seasoned pro. Still, it came under the heading of gradual improvement, and Tiger sensed a pride in her gathering accomplishments. "The typewriter is your friend." That's what had been written in the little booklet that accompanied her Christmas present from Daddy four years ago. That particular typewriter wasn't *really* a friend. It wasn't even a casual acquaintance. It was more of a total stranger. And by Easter it had evolved into a venal enemy. But that was long ago…and *this* typewriter, an electric job, was trying very hard to be friendly. It didn't jam. It didn't shake or make disconsolate noises. It just hummed happily and was very patient, even with Tiger's erratic pace. It was an all-around *simpatico* good fellow, a chum, a buddy. And so Tiger devoted even her lunch hour toward the further cementing of their purring-good relationship.

Martha had asked Tiger to join some of the girls for lunch, a humanitarian gesture that Tiger just wasn't up to. Besides, that glazed doughnut was lying in her stomach like a chunk of fermenting brain coral, ebbing and flowing in a surf of coffee that had a caffeine count so high that she was in danger of eternal insomnia, even after death. Necroinsomnia. Play *that* on your Smith-Corona.

Anyway, by the time Martha and the other *femmes*

returned from their jabbering lunch, Tiger had taken her tatta-tat-tat and fashioned it into a rather acceptable pa-tumn, pa-tumn, pa-tumn.

Martha came over. "How you doing?"

"Fine. It's all coming back to me." Then Tiger looked at the 424 misspellings. "Maybe tomorrow it'll come back in English."

Martha sounded like the Harvard football coach. "Hang in there. You'll get it." And she went back to her own machine.

Tiger stayed at her machine, rather satisfied with the way it was going. After all—*Roam wasn't bilt in a dae.* The coffee was at low tide, and the doughnut had receded with it, nestling up somewhere in Tiger's intestines, where, in spite of the fact that it was lying dormant, she knew she'd hear from it later. Tiger glanced up at the big clock without breaking stride. She wasn't normally a clock watcher, but everyone was leaving. The other girls were covering their machines as though the things had just died. Martha was standing next to her. "Five o'clock. We've been sprung."

"That late?" Yes. And all the girls were going through the doorway in threes—mini, midi, maxi—soon disappearing down the elevator shafts. And tomorrow a new batch would ascend, serve their time, and at five o'clock go down the shaft in a like manner. Continuity. The life cycle. Evolution. And Tiger was a part of it, and it was comforting.

"Which way do you go?" Martha asked.

"Well...I think I'll stay a little longer. Is that okay?"

"Sure, but don't make it a habit. And if you stay past five thirty, don't forget to sign the check-out book in the lobby."

"Okay."

"Night, Janice."

"Good night and…thanks."

Martha turned back and smiled. Then she exited with the rest of the herd.

And so it was just the three of them. Smith, Corona & Her. She worked awhile longer, feeling the knowledge coursing through her fingers. It was like swimming and riding a bike—you don't forget. You always have it. Conditioned responses. But as the clock sneaked up on five thirty, she felt a slight insecurity that would shortly develop into a roaring panic. She hated it in herself, but she had so disenfranchised herself from the world in general that the prospect of signing the check-out book shook her up. Where would it be in that big lobby? Who would be in charge of it, an SS man? How could she identify herself as an employee? She had no proof, no card, no button. No indelible ink stamp on her wrist that read "H, d & M." How easy it would be for her to be accused of burglary. How simple for the SS man to explain that he shot the girl because she had run past him without either identifying herself or calling out the standard password: "What is right for General Motors is right for America." No, she decided, she'd have to be out of there by the witching hour.

She covered her typewriter affectionately. Good job, old paint. Then she walked to and waited by the elevator, thinking about her new friend, Martha. Martha would introduce her around, into a straight environment, a contemporary scene, *sans* pot and passions. There'd be beer and hamburgers. Men named George. Apartments with wallpaper. (Maybe Martha needed a roommate. But it was a bit early for that because maybe Martha was a slob or a dyke or a chronic crier.) Old movies. Bogart. Records, antique hunting. People across a hall you could borrow a cup of sanity from. Letters from home. (Of course, to *get* a letter, you must first *send* one.) The point was—anything was possible. Tiger was riding a glorious high. She had survived her first day on the job, her first day without what's his name. And now she was going back to her cheery little room at the nice YWCA. She passed through the lobby without any trouble because it was not yet five thirty and no password was required. An idea struck her as she reached the street and she acted on it immediately…

…And came out of the Rent Anything store with a portable electric typewriter. Not a great one but a good one, in good condition, a machine that knew its way around the language. At $6 a week it wasn't a bad deal. She was making $75. But why they called the damned thing portable—it had to weigh fifty pounds in its bare feet. All that made it portable was that it had a handle. By that kind of thinking, one could put a handle on a DC-9 and carry it aboard a 747 because it would be "portable." No matter. She listed to port until she was able to find a cab. The cabby was then good enough to wait at a Take-Out-Sandwich place. And when she arrived at the Marshal House Y, it was with a typewriter in one hand, neatly balanced by a heroic sandwich in the other—a sandwich that had everything in it, including its creator's admiring good wishes. All that kept the sandwich from overcompensating for the typewriter was that Tiger had taken a small bite of it on the long voyage home. That had evened things out. But the bite dropped, like a prodigious rock, into her stomach, breaking up forever the glazed doughnut that was still lying there like an iron fist, gathering rust and twittering like a raw nerve ending.

She set up the typewriter so that it received the best light in the room. Since she had neglected to buy typewriting paper, she would have to do her stuff on Marshal House Y stationery, which had limitations mostly because it was lavender blue and silly-dilly, also narrow, and short, and bulky, and floral. But it was better than toilet tissue, of which there was such a goodly supply that Tiger had to wonder if the former occupant of 1224 hadn't gone out in a blaze of dysentery.

She finished the hero sandwich right down to the last clump of garlic. And with it she polished off the two bottles of ginger ale that she had brought it for companionship. Later she figured she'd go out for a walk, pick up a paper, grab an orange drink at Nedick's, and return to her room for a good night's sleep, the better to face the next day with.

And so, with spirits high and tummy full, she sat down at the typewriter and listened to it purr. It was noisier than the one at the office, but in its favor was the fact no one was watching her. The first thing she typed on three pages of the ladylike stationery was, quite necessarily, cathartic: *"My name is Janice Lynn McAllister, and I am, I think, of sound mind. I am basically from just outside Indianapolis, but, in general, I belong to the world. I will destroy this letter in a moment because, as long as I'm on the subject of me, it is about to get just a teensy bit raunchy. I feel a need to think sexy here because it has always been my main hang-up. I would like to meet, please, a man who will properly fill both my mind and my body. A man not too big but, please, not too lacking where it counts. I make good love now, much better than I used to, and certainly better than any girl just outside Indianapolis, or inside for that matter. I don't consider myself soiled because, what* the hell, times have changed. I consider myself experienced, traveled, knowledgeable. I know what turns me on, and I know how to do likewise with whoever I'm socking it to. I'm not exactly aggressive or even terribly original. But I'm not just submissive either. I think I'm responsive. I think I can be inventive, too. I think I'll try anything, but, sorry, the lights have to be out. When the lights are on, I begin to notice things like pictures and lamps and they kill my concentration. If it's dark, I can make my own pictures and they ain't bad. And though I don't consider myself a wanton, to be honest, I would like, just once, to wrap myself around a man who can do me real good and not feel he has to talk about it or even refer to it when we're finished. I think, in those circumstances, I can really let myself go, really tear up the sheets and steam up the windows. That goes for language, too. I'd like to go nutty and yell obscenities all over the place. I'd like to say "fuck" and "suck" and all the words because I think they help heighten the passion. Only, when it's over, I don't want to discuss it. I don't want to be reminded that I was good or wild or crazy. I just want to go to a museum and look at Klee or a library and read Montaigne. I want to keep all reference to sex out of my daily life because, Jesus, I think I'm shy. Also, thanks to Mom and Dad, I guess I still feel that sex is dirty. By doing it in the dark, I can pretend it's not me. But if I talk about it in the daytime, that is me, and all I want to do is what I want to do and not feel that God is going to strike me dead. Daylight is Janice. Darkness is Tiger. In darkness I can allow a man to say, "I love your cunt." If he said that to me in daylight, I would dissolve. In darkness, then, I will be the craziest, sickest, wildest female a man ever got hold of. In daylight, the best I can ever be is an escaped nun. Therefore, and in conclusion, once I establish myself as an independent wage earner, I am going to devote a good deal of my time and effort to finding someone who will be Little Boy Blue when we're in church, but who, when the sun goes

*down, will do likewise. And I he. And then he me again. And Me
Thee, and tee-hee. And when he's in me, I want to just spin around on
him until he fires me at the moon. I want him to have a prick as alive
as his mind. I want him to stab me with passion every night and——"*

The phone rang. She kept writing.

"During the day he will be a companion and a teacher and a——"

It kept ringing. She kept writing, or trying.

"friend, friend. Someone who will worry about me and——"

The telephone was not of a mind to stop. So Tiger stopped.
And her heart came very close to failing because reality was
about to get through to her and ruin the great snow job
she was performing on herself. Reality with its incessant
ringing. She removed the page on which she was typing and
crumpled it. Then she crumpled the other two pages that
had preceded it, somehow feeling that whoever was on the
other end of the phone, once she'd picked up the receiver,
he'd be able to read the dirty things she had written. She
picked up the receiver and didn't feel very good.

"Yes?" she said. "Hello, Luther. Fine, and you? Yes,
I'm breathing better now. Yes, I got a job. I'm a typist. I
can too type. I can too spell. Yes, I miss you. No, I don't
want to come back. Maybe not ever. Maybe never, I don't
know. I'm sorry, but that scene with Fat, it just wiped me
out. Luther, I'm only gone one day. I don't *know* where I
belong. I'm trying to find out. I have *not* forgotten what you
look like. You're the one with the big eye in the middle of his
forehead, right? Luther, *please!* I am trying to *evolve!* Now I've
crawled up out of the…the primordial ooze, and I'm hoping

to grow legs. If it turns out that they don't work, then okay, I'll wriggle back to you and complete my degeneration. But in the meantime, you have to leave me *alone!*...Sir? Sir? You have a wrong number, sir. Please hang up and call the zoo. This is a goddamned recording." She slammed down the receiver very hard and was surprised to see how upset she was.

Then the crying came. Deep and gasping again. And she wondered if the whole problem wasn't that she was allergic to Luther. If she was, then she'd been taking the wrong pills. She crawled slowly into bed but knew that she'd never sleep. Somewhere in the middle of the night, drenched within an overwhelming self-pity, she got out of bed and wrote a letter home for close to three hours. Then, without reading it, she signed it "Louisa May Alcott" and tore it up. After that she got two hours of sleep. Two hours—it was getting to be her average.

I could tell she was upset; only, I didn't really know why. What the hell, I'd given her a whole day to see how dumb she was acting. Besides, it was no picnic for me, either. Fat and Leon gave me a pretty wide berth that day. As a matter of actual fact, they were out all day long and didn't fly in until well past midnight, and even then I barely heard them. Maybe they were afraid I was going to tell them to move the hell out, ass and baggage. But to send them packing before Tiger came back would just have to stick out like some kind of concession. She'd realize how badly I wanted her back and how I'd do just about anything to get her back—and that, of course, would signal the oncoming end. Leon knocked on my door at 3 A.M. All he wanted to do was say *au revoir*. Which he did, just like that. Au revoir. *As if he were a goddamn legionnaire going off to fight in the Sahara. No speech, no thanks, no apologies, just* au revoir. *Maybe the son of a bitch was French, who knew? I didn't know where the hell he was going, but then, I didn't know where the fuck he came from either. Therefore, nothing had been lost because nothing had been gained in the first place. (Philosophical Observation No. 63, from the Memoirs of Daffy Duck.) The next morning Fat told me he'd be leaving, too, just as soon as his cleaning came back. Everybody was walking out on me. Everybody except my toys. My toys, bless 'em, they were loyal. If a man has a couple of good toys in life, he can muddle through. I had a soldier, and a doggie, and a teddy, and a mouse in a car, and a bunny on a bike, and a man on a wagon—companions all. I didn't have my wounded ballet dancer doll. The bad girl who came to visit—she stole it. I really did miss it. And while I was missing it, the goddamn New York Telephone Company showed up and took my toy phone away. Which meant I couldn't even call Nanny again. I chewed on my pacifier and wet my diaper. I wasn't supposed to do that. I'd really get it for that.*

16

Tiger's next day was a little easier. And that surprised her. She'd lain awake practically all night, dreading the next day so much that, when it finally camped on her windowsill, it shimmered not with dread but with relief. If nothing else, it marked an end to night, and that was a good night to have an end marked to. And yet—why was she all that upset? Luther's call did not come exactly as a surprise. Also, he'd be calling again. And though she hated him for not letting her rest, she also delighted in his keeping in touch as she slalomed her way through her old, yet alien world. The best strategy would be, she reasoned, to act unconcerned when he called. That would burn him more than anything. The next time he called she'd say, "Oh, hi—I've been expecting your call. How are you...Lenny?" She smiled. She liked that. That had style. That was the old spirit. Rah-rah.

Before checking in at work, she made certain to have a good and well-balanced breakfast, to compensate for her lack of sleep. And what better place than Schrafft's, where they had all those cute little rolls? It wasn't something she'd be able to do every day on her salary, but since it was early on in a new game, she figured it was right and necessary to fortify and pamper herself just a trifle. French toast, please. *Très magnifique.*

The work was placed on her desk like straw for Rumpelstiltskin. She attacked and performed admirably. She also handled the coffee break with more assurance, barking her order to the counterman in the hole, who threw it at her with a slight curve, but she was ready and one-handed it like Johnny Bench.

Lunch was with Martha, just the two of them, exchanging life stories. She made no mention of Luther, making up instead a huge dramatic story about a back-street romance with a man of forty-eight who was dying of a war wound. He was divorced, of course, and had three children, two of them older than Tiger. Also, he wanted to marry her before he died, which looked to be coming in the spring. It was a much better story than Martha had to tell because Martha for all her basic intelligence, was from a large family in Brooklyn and nothing ever happened there except periodic unemployment for her father who was a steamfitter or something—but a good one. So Tiger did most of the talking. And she was quite adept at the tale telling, almost as good as Luther might have been under similar circumstances. Tom Dietrich (Tiger made him up) seemed so real that she actually found herself sobbing into the soup of the day, which was watered-down enough. Martha advised her to break up with Tom as soon as possible because it wasn't fair to either of them. Also, it would leave a big scar on Tiger's subconscious. Tiger allowed as to how right Martha was but wondered if she could stand not seeing Tom ever again. Also, she wanted to be with him when he died. Martha cried for Tom but still placed Tiger's well-being first, and suggested that Tiger try to meet new men. What new men? Where? Martha knew a few. She'd work on it.

It rained exceptionally hard that afternoon, the rain plinking so loud on the exterior glass walls that it could be heard over the typing. But Tiger liked it. It was cleansing. She wondered if the Lever Brothers Building, not too far away, didn't lather in such a downpour. Or if the Seagram's Building didn't get drunk. Or if the Arrow Shirt Building (there just *had* to be one) didn't shrink. Or if the Yacht Club Building didn't float away.

It was really pouring on the street, splattering like transparent plums. And the ever-revolving door kept depositing people from the lobby into the rain, where they stacked up under the overhanging canopy, knowing that to venture further would be like going full fathom five.

A few people had umbrellas and decided to walk for their lives. The rest just stood around and said "Wow." Scrambling for cabs would prove nothing except that people in crises were basically ornery. Tiger stood there as helpless as the others, only not as bothered because she was in no great hurry to get back to the Y. She looked at the people and wanted to tell them to take to the high ground; only she didn't think it would get much of a laugh. She had no umbrella, no raincoat, and there was no chance of the rain's stopping for forty days and nights. A bus pulled to the curb a little up the street. Tiger couldn't see, but she knew that two of everything were getting on. Two chickens, two apes, two goats, too much.

A cab splashed up right before her, and its doors swung open even before the cab had stopped. A man's voice gurgled out at the crowd. "Come on! Get in!" A dozen daring girls shrieked and raced for the open door, and Tiger thought that people get killed at soccer games like that. "No! No!" said the voice, and an index finger stuck out and pointed straight at Tiger's heart. "You!"

Tiger pointed to herself like a disbelieving Miss America. "Me?"

"Yes, you! Come on!"

The other girls groaned, and Tiger felt guilty. Why her? But while she was cogitating a hand reached out and she found herself almost flying into the cab.

She looked at the man alongside her. A pipe smoker. Around forty. Handsome in a menacing, cocksure way. Probably tall. The man pulled the door shut, and the cab pulled away. The man looked at Tiger and smiled. "Hello."

Tiger organized herself as best she could under such short notice. She looked only once at the man and smiled back, instantly determining that she might have made a mistake in getting in, and that if she wasn't careful, it could just turn out to be a very bumpy ride. She tried to see if the driver was a criminal type, but his head was turned full away. For all she knew she was about to be driven upstate, raped, robbed, and murdered. Served her right.

The man was enjoying his momentary advantage. He puffed big clouds of pipe smoke into the cab with the obvious intention of overwhelming her with irresistible aromatic masculinity. Tiger resented the tactic and coughed on purpose. A nice, juicy, watery cough, something of the consumptive—just in case he had any ideas of sticking his tongue down her dying throat.

The man failed to get the message. He removed the pipe from his mouth and spoke with superb modulation. God, she hated him. "Wet?"

She brushed off some rain and would be struck dead before she'd make the mewing noises of a damsel rescued. "Yes. I perspire heavily."

The man didn't quite know what to make of that, so he laughed loudly. Then he raised his eyebrows in that saccharine knowing smile. "Does the pipe bother you?"

"Oh, no, no, no." Then she coughed again. Louder. Then she waved her hands about to disperse the heavy billows. "It's all right. It's fine."

Because she had said that it was all right, the man (an obvious moron) kept puffing away. Tiger could not believe how ridiculous he was in that Aquascutum trench coat surrounded by Dunhill pipe smoke. And damned if he didn't nudge her with his elbow and wink and say, "Always get into cabs with strangers?"

Actually it was a good question. Why *had* she gotten into the cab? Did she think he was Luther? Or poor expiring Tom Dietrich? Or Clark Gable? Did she think it was her father come from Indianapolis on a white horse? Or did she think it was a total stranger and did that idea tickle her? Or did she not think at all, which was more apt to be the case, judging from her behavior over the last few days. It was certainly something to ponder in her old age, provided she ever arrived there. The odds, though, were in favor of her checking out early…and the very cab she was in could easily be the vehicle that would take her to her demise. Not that she any longer believed that the man was a threat, but more because the visibility outside was so absurdly limited that it had to be definitely suicidal to…

"I asked if you always get into cabs with strangers?"

"Always," she said. The trick, she knew, was to agree the man to death. It was a philosophy that Smith girls used when wanting to dampen the ardor of an undesirable suitor. It was invariably successful, though, once, the Amherst man she was working it on had his hand halfway up her goose-pimpling thigh before saying, "Ah, shit," and walking away.

"I see," the man beside her said. The *hell* he saw. He puffed three times, three clouds north, and the cabby disappeared within them and, for a moment, all there was of the driver was a series of Morse coughs. The man, undaunted (but then, so are idiots), tried again. "We work for the same firm, you and I. I saw you in the commissary, and because I liked what I saw, I asked who you were."

She didn't comment. He hadn't asked a question; therefore, no answer was required.

"Is that okay?" he asked.

That was definitely a question, so she answered with a masterful disinterest. "Okay."

It had to have been about that time that the man began to realize that he was not doing well with his wet waif. So, with utter charm, he puffed up another atomic mushroom and asked, "Wouldn't you like to know who *I* am?"

"No."

The man, not an idiot in the true sense, knew when he was being stiffed. Struck silent by her passionate disinterest, he puffed so hard on his pipe that even *he* coughed. They *all* coughed. It was like a tuberculosis ward in Geneva. There was so much smoke in the cab that, from the outside, it must have looked as though it were on fire. Tiger, not caring for asphyxia as an end to all woe, rolled down her window just a trifle…and the smoke raced out so quickly, and with such a wind, that had she not held hard to the door handle, she might have been sucked out with it. She wasn't certain, but she thought that perhaps the man went flying past her, siphoned out through the partially opened window. But no such luck. He was still there in the swirling Kansas twister, still sitting like Lincoln at his memorial; only now he was taking extreme umbrage and his voice was expressing high dudgeon. "Where can I drop you?"

Tiger leaned forward, fanning a clearing so that she could find the cabby's ear. "The Marshal House Y, please. It's on East Forty-seventh Street." Then she leaned back, having taken note of the driver's name in the undulating mist. It was a thing Luther always did, collected names. In this case the man's name was not worth recording. "Robert E. Williams." Forget it.

The smoke was on the rise in the cab, for the man was about to try his charm again, once more into the breach. "I could have let you drown, you know."

"I know."

"Maybe next time I will."

"I know."

"You're a little bitch. You won't last a week."

"I know."

The man shouted to the cabby, a great cliché, but what else was there to be said? "Step on it, will you?"

The driver said, "I know." And Tiger laughed to herself. Good old Robert E. Williams, true to his breed, had been eavesdropping all along and had, with royal impertinence, delivered unto the Aquascutum man, the final put-down. Cheers, oh, cabby, and may all your tips be big ones.

The cab moored in front of the Y, and the curb was at the man's side. Tiger noticed his hands, wiggling on his knees. What were they about to do—pinch or punch? She decided not to risk it and got out of the cab on her side. For her troubles she was close to flattened by a truck that cursed as it whooshed by. She turned to the man and said, "Thank you," before closing the door on him, she hoped, for all time. But if the man ever said, "You're welcome," she never heard it because of all the loud smoke.

She scampered behind the idling cab, taking no chances, and galomped through the puddles and up the steps to the entrance of the Y. And there she bumped into Luther.

He stood in the hard and vertical rain, thoroughly drenched. It was difficult for Tiger to make him out because the rain was cascading off her own eyelashes in such a manner as to make it seem as though she were looking at Luther through a beaded curtain. "Luther?"

His collar was up, his hair a tangled black doormat, and he was very, very disturbed with her as he stood blocking her entrance. "Where have you been? Your mother and I have been frantic. We even checked the bus terminal. And the morgue. We want you to come home, Beverly. Your old room is ready. And Mr. Hinckley says you can have your old job back at the shirt factory."

Tiger had expected that if she ever saw Luther again, her heart would go out of its mind. It hadn't. Therefore she was relieved and disheartened simultaneously. Perhaps it was as they said (*who* said?), you can't look back. All she could feel was the cold rain going right through her, trickling down her legs and gathering in her shoes. "Can we get out of the rain?"

"What rain?"

She pushed past him and into the lobby, where a pool of water formed so quickly about her feet that, for a moment, she had the disquieting feeling that, like the wicked witch in the Wizard of Oz, she was melting.

Luther came in behind her, shaking his jacket free of the veil of rain and looking around at the large and gloomy lobby. "Take my advice, Jessica. Get out of this house tonight. The ghost of Jeremy Dalton is in these very walls."

She faced him, unperturbed. Seeing him again had not proved as shattering as she had anticipated. Seeing him, by God, was easier than *thinking* him. Seeing him alive and as wet as she was seemed to reduce the pressure that had been building inside her since the moment she left him. A big truck tire in her tummy was slowly deflating. She could feel the hiss of it, and she relaxed in the slackening tension. "I'm not doing any more movies, Luther. From now on all my dialogue is spontaneous—though sometimes a little repetitious like...leave me alone." She liked the way she had said that. Forthright, unhesitating. No vacillating. No crap.

Luther was a forlorn thing. How long had he been standing in the rain in order for everything on him to have turned so monocolored and sopping gray? He looked like a man on a breadline who had just been told that the last two crusts of bread had been awarded to a man who had the last piece of ham. "I *have* left you alone," he said. "For almost forty-eight hours. It's not working. Too much too soon. I'm getting the bends."

She walked away from him, across the lobby to the

elevator, which wasn't there, so she rang for it and waited with her back to Luther. She heard his squishy shoes come to a stop behind her. She turned, and without looking at him, she made an imaginary line on the floor with her shoe tip. "You can't go past this line. If you do, you get electrocuted."

He smiled, seeming to respect her threat. Then he came directly to the point. "Leon the Rodent is gone. He got depressed and threw himself under a cat. *Fat* goes as soon as his wardrobe comes back from the laundry." He was standing five feet away from her with his heart opened. "Tiger, the longer I let you stay away, the better the chances you'll forget you were brought up by us wolf people. You'll be walking on your hind legs in no time, and that'll be the end of it."

The elevator arrived, its door opening automatically. "I'm sorry," she said, and stepped into the elevator and pressed twelve. He moved smoothly, stopping the door from closing by letting it continually push against his big shoulder. The door pushed, retreated, pushed, retreated… but he took the gentle hammering while just standing there looking at her. She said it without concern about whether he lived or died or got pressed into a man nine feet tall and six inches wide: "You're not allowed up. This is a girls' hotel."

"Oh, that poor girl."

"Luther, please. I'll call you." She was being patronizing. She hated people who patronized, so she hated herself, but she still patronized. "I really will. I'll call you first chance."

"Can't. They took the phone back. Don Ameche and his gang of ruffians."

"I'll send word."

"How?"

"The queen's ring."

"The queen is dead."

"Pigeons."

"You don't have any."

"I'll get some."

"You won't."

"I will...*Luther!* Will you get *out* of here!" She was furious. Her back was pressed hard against the elevator panel, and if he took but one step toward her she'd scream and kick and God help him. She hated him. She was glad he showed up the way he did because it proved to her that where absence made the heart grow fonder, presence only made it stop cold. Her fists were clenched, and she had chewed so hard into her lower lip that she could taste blood.

He took a moment, to monitor her wrath and to consider what it was that he actually wanted. He smiled, but it faded hurriedly. He started to speak, but the words never found their way past his muddled censor. Finally, he stepped aside, allowing the elevator door to close. And it looked to him like a sideways guillotine, slicing into Tiger, then obliterating her. He stared at the closed door and listened to the elevator going up. He stayed where he was until he heard the elevator stop somewhere up there. Satisfied that she had arrived safely, he turned and squished across the lobby, retracing his own soggy footprints as though it were the only way he could find his way out. He stopped at the desk, where the ancient lady in charge had been watching the entire scene. And when he spoke to her, it was with a conspiratorial tone. "Anything happens to that girl, I'll hold you responsible. She's had five heart transplants and two knee operations already. How much is she expected to take?" He left, stepping into the downpour as the old lady wondered just what in the world he was.

Well, that *didn't work. Maybe it was the weather. Whatever it was, my appearance at the Y went over like Hitler playing Grossinger's. I had actually convinced myself that after a couple of days away from me, she'd come a-running into my swarthy arms at the very sight of me. Shows you how wrong you can be if you really try hard enough. Still, if I was any judge of the female nature, she had reacted just a little too strongly to my showing up in that DAR outhouse. Had she been cool, had she been controlled all the way, I'd have been concerned. But the fact that she ended up screaming at me, well, I took that to be an expression of interest. The opposite of love is disinterest—not hate. Love and hate come out of the same stable. They carry the same colors. One may be Cain and the other Abel, but they're still Siamese in their twinness. Disinterest, on the other hand, is a cold loner and a distant cousin. Whereas indifference, that icy son of a bitch, he is a great and frosty aunt, twelve times removed and on your mother's side. Speaking of mother, I still hadn't heard a word from her. They were obviously spending the best part of their vacation not writing to me. There were so many others they could not write to, why did they have to pick me out? Small wonder I kept wetting my bed. I was sublimating, convincing myself I was riding a surfboard right up to the Hawaiian sands on which they were lying around sucking coconuts and getting leid. Oh, well, and what the hell...what was really bothering me was that Tiger had gotten out of a cab in which some guy had brought her to the Y. And I didn't care for that one iota in hell. Two days away, and she's got a guy at the Y. (Rhyme time, folks.) I don't mind a girl walking out on me in the dead of the stinking night while I'm up to my dingoes with* a freaked-out weirdo. I don't even mind never seeing her again if that's the way she wants it. But what I do object to is another guy being immediately called in to cut my time. I expect any girl who leaves me to be discriminating enough to remain celibate for at least a week. I expect her to "think convent" until my memory has properly cooled. I expect her to serve penitence and crush grapes and maybe bake a little bread with a gay monk. What I do not expect her to do is to instantly hook up with a priest with the sole intention of humping him on the altar in the Y. You know what goes on in those Y's. Those priests, they come in to hear prayers and to give solace and they end up with more ass than a cop taking kickbacks in a red-light district. It's true in YWHA's, too. Don't think for a minute that the rabbi on duty doesn't get himself a nifty bit of ass from the ladies of the Hadassah. Think of the very word: "Hadassah." Break it down into syllables, and you come up with the ancient rabbinical sex chant: "Had-Ass-Ah!" Anyway, regardless of one's religious persuasions, you have to admit that there's an awful lot of hanky-panky going on in the name of the Lord. So I didn't much care for Tiger taking up with a clergyman in a cab as she was doing, probably going down on him in return for some kind of supreme unction, while he genuflects her little boobs with one hand while investigating her sweet box with the other. I don't care—whoever the bloke in question was— Father Divine, Father Christmas, or Mother Russia—the situation was too quickly getting out of hand and bore watching because the whole damned history of the Judeo-Christian church has been one of demonic debauchery in the Lord's name. Just keep in mind the fact that the attitude of a good atheist is "Fuck God." Whereas the attitude of the church is "Fuck everyone." For myself, pals, all I wanted to do was "fuck Tiger" as in days of yore. Therefore, plans had to be made, traps set, the pit baited. For it is written in the Koran that the race goes to the quick. And as even a schoolboy knows, time and Tiger wait for no man. Amen, and how's your ass?

17

Another restless night for Tiger, and she was glad to see the end of it. She wanted an end to her affair with Luther, too. For that's what it had been—an affair. Not a relationship. Not a love. An affair, and with all that the word implied. Transitory. Migrant. Ugly. Salacious. So good riddance to it. She found herself thinking about Luther in the past tense. That was good. Perhaps he was truly behind her. Now if he'd only stay out of the way, she could press on. Now whatever he did with his life, it was his own foolish business. She'd be damned if she'd let him louse up *her* life any more than he already had. And she meant that. That was not just a silly observation. That was a cast-iron vow.

She arrived at the office about as unsmiling as she'd ever been. Martha identified the man in yesterday's cab. Gerald du Bois, middle son of Harper, du Bois & Mallory. Tiger was as unimpressed with the man's identity as she had been with his personality. Martha said, "Tsk-tsk," but Tiger said, "So what?"

She was ready to plow into her work, confident that she would do it better today than yesterday. Nothing would stand in her way. She sat down at her typewriter in the steno pool, and there was a note in its carriage: "See me, please." And it had scrawled signature, illegible, and an imprinted name: "F. D. Douglas." (Again with the initials.) Tiger asked Martha who F. D. Douglas was and Martha replied, "Chief talent scout and watch out for the couch."

Tiger got the message but just couldn't believe that, in this day and age, men in offices still behaved in so archaic a manner. Besides, there were a few girls, though not many, laboring in the steno pool who Tiger thought were immediately more provocative than she herself. Why hadn't F. D. Douglas, the old roué, chosen one of them? To which Martha replied, "He already has."

So armed, Tiger walked to F. D. Douglas' office, determined to make a fool of the cad even if it meant losing her job. She wondered about the true meaning of Martha's statement. Had the man *had* all those girls, or had he just *tried* all those girls? And *which* of all those girls felt the cushions of that couch on her back? And how did they benefit from their experience? And what in the world was *she*, Janice McAllister, neo-virgin, doing walking into such a pseudo-slapstick situation? Perhaps it was all a Cocteau dream. Perhaps she should not go and should just quit. But she was too curious and angry. And she also found it so ridiculous that she had to stifle the giggles before going beyond the door with the "F. D. Douglas" on it.

Fred Derek Douglas' office was perfect. It smacked of status, yet was not opulent. It had windows all over the place, and its own john, and a small bar, and plush chairs, and a huge desk, and Fred Douglas—an athletic forty-five-year-old man who presided over it all in shirt sleeves and loosened tie. The whole effect was of a magnificently confident lawyer, well in command of his own comet, undeniably handsome in face and form, and not a man that any sane girl could find too many reasons for resisting.

But even as he spoke, Tiger sensed a dichotomy about the man, an off-center quality that undoubtedly served him well in his legal combats but that could frightfully unnerve any young girl under his scrutiny. He was overpoweringly direct in his statements, yet he never really looked at her. He seemed to operate via oblique tangents and puzzling digressions. More, he had a practiced glibness that seemed to portray a total lack of interest in the humanity of the person he was talking to. In short, he was something she'd have to contend with.

"There won't be all that much dictation, Miss—what's your name, please?"

"McAllister."

"Mostly it'll be straight typing. Depositions, briefs, research, memos. It *can* be a lot of work, but it doesn't call for any legal training. Also, it's fifteen dollars a week more than you're now getting and you have your own office." He tossed the rest of it away. "It's small, but it's private, and a lot better than working in that noisy bullpen."

Tiger looked off to the side. There was the small office. It was neat, tidy, and had no door except the one leading into F.D.'s office. Also, it had a couch. A nice, big *couch*. "That office?" she asked.

"Yes." He kept very busy, never looking up.

"And it only opens into here, right?"

"Correct."

"And it doesn't open into out *there*—just into here." She felt as though she were doing a guest appearance on *The Carol Burnett Show.*

He looked up and smiled. His wild blue eyes jigged happily because he sensed that she was onto him, and he liked that because it made it all spicier. "Yes, only into in here."

And she knew that he was onto her, so she figured she'd just play it full out Zazu Pitts and let the chips fall where they may. "That's a nice couch, sir."

"Thank you."

"I'll bet it opens into a nice bed."

"As a matter of fact, it does. Like to see a demonstration?"

"Oh, no, sir. Please don't bother."

"It's no bother." But he didn't bother to get up and bother.

Now Tiger became more dangerous. Arlene Dahl staving off Ricardo Montalban. "How many notches in the mattress?"

That got him. "Pardon?"

"How many have you bagged?"

He really liked her more than he had even anticipated. "Three thousand four hundred fifty-three and a half."

"A half?"

"A minor. I threw her back."

And damned if she didn't like him, which was obviously his plan, so beware. "I hear that girls who come to work for you are never seen again. Is that true?"

He turned a silver-framed photograph toward her. It was of a very chic ash blond lady about forty. "Exhibit A. I happen to be a very happily married man."

Tiger figured she was losing ground and creating the wrong impression. So she resorted to ye olde caustic candor. "And I happen to be the worst typist in the world. So why pick *me* out?"

"You already know. It's the tradition."

"Not where I come from."

"And where do you come from?"

"Wherever I'm going back to when I leave here." She started out.

"Hey. Don't be dumb." He was standing.

"I don't want to be disrespectful, Mr. Douglas, but really I think you've got the wrong girl."

"Oh, cut it out." He was laughing, and he looked good laughing. "You're perfectly capable of taking care of yourself. And in spite of the things you may have heard, no one has yet done anything on my couch against his or her will."

"His?"

"Legal terminology." He had that way about him, of seeming to lose ground, only to snap back, so that he owned more. "Now, come on. Let's make it twenty-five a week more. I think you're a *great* typist. Is it a deal?"

Tiger tried to be logical, but the man had literally turned her into whipped cream and without half trying. She allowed as to that happening because she was basically nineteen and painfully ill equipped to exchange barbs with a master. She added it up in her mind. Twenty-five a week would bring her salary to a hundred, a nice round figure. Of course, accepting the job implied that she also accepted the couch, and that could be dangerous, in spite of the fact that Fred Douglas didn't look so sex-starved that he'd take her against her will.

Anyway, all things considered, she decided to go for broke. "It's a deal." But she would try to establish an understanding well ahead of any incident. "Just one question."

"Yes?"

"Is it all right if every now and then you *lose* a case?"

"Certainly."

"Good."

"Only it doesn't happen too often." And he added, "You know the phrase 'habeas corpus'? It means 'we have the body.'"

Tiger countered, "And do *you* know the phrase 'habeas shmabeas'?"

"No."

"Neither do I. But it's something to think about." She left the office with a smile, but he was laughing uproariously. And she wasn't sure whether or not she wasn't getting in over her head. Still, somehow she felt that it was absurdly unreal to think that that man, that beautiful sexy man, would feel compelled to wrestle her down onto the couch. And then it dawned on her that he might never *have* to. That was his strategy. Create the environment, establish the threat, make one small move—and watch, folks, how the lady topples over onto her back because that's what she wanted to do in the *first* place. It was like that guy Luther had told her about. The one who'd invite a girl into his apartment and then leave the room. And then he'd observe her through a secret opening and watch how she reacted to the pornographic photographs he had lying about. If she picked them up and studied them, figuring no one was watching, he was "in." But if she immediately put them down in disgust, he was "out." Simple. And it was reputed to have worked every time. Therefore, she was onto Fred Douglas and his evil plot, and she'd be ready; only why was she trembling? Could it be that it was all *fait accompli*? Had she already taken the last step and sealed her doom by simply taking the first step? Tune in tomorrow, folks, and watch the smart-assed Janice McAllister get *hers*—but with a very handsome man, you bet.

She moved into her new office (the one with the *couch*) within the hour. Martha didn't know quite what to make of it. She just hadn't figured Janice McAllister to be that kind of girl. Tiger explained as best she could: that she figured that twenty-five extra dollars a week was worth the risk and that, as far as she could see, Fred Douglas was not all that formidable, and that she could handle him, etc., etc. Martha smiled and voiced the opinion that Tiger would have ample opportunity to prove the veracity of her theory.

The first ample opportunity arose at 5 P.M. that very day, when Tiger brought in the work that Fred had given her to type up that morning. He was glad to see her and neatly closed the door behind her like a shifty matador. When she turned to see him, he was gone. All that there was was the sound of the lock clicking closed. And she knew instinctively: "It is now post time."

A drink was thrust out at her, accompanied by a resonant masculine voice. "I figure you like scotch. Now then…let's see what kind of typing you do." She watched *his* hand take the papers from *her* hand, and again the male voice came. "Make yourself comfortable, Janice."

Boy, was he ever fast. She had yet to say a word—and there she was, locked in and balancing a straight scotch that had to be drugged. She put it down noiselessly.

Without looking up, the male in the room knew that

she had put it down. "Don't like scotch? Try something else. Help yourself."

She looked over at the bar. Suddenly she wanted a Yoo-Hoo. Or a Bosco. Or maybe she could come alive with a Coke. How about a sarsaparilla, little girl? Or maybe a jug of Demerol to slow your racing heart. "If you don't mind—" She didn't care for how weak in the knees that sounded, but the words were gone and there was no reeling them back.

"Oh, come on," he said, still not looking up from the papers. "None of it's poisoned...Well, a couple small typos, but not a bad job. Not bad at all, Janice. You can fix it up in the morning." He was walking toward her. She hadn't even seen him get up, yet there he was, walking toward her. He could skip moves, like time-lapse photography. She'd have to watch that. "How'd you like your first day on the job with evil old me?"

He was standing in front of her with his delft blue eyes, so damned sure of himself. And yet, she thought, he's pleasant and attractive. He's bright and kind of charming. He's desirable as hell, and isn't this 1971? And aren't I a healthy girl? And is that not a sturdy couch? Ya, dass iss a sturdy couch.

"You faint in this office, and you're fired." His eyes were leaping into her eyes, and she knew that all the color had abandoned her face. And she puzzled over why she should feel all that weak. "Jesus," he said, "you *are* going to faint."

"I'm all right," piped her midget voice, and she was suddenly terrified that a man could affect her in such a manner. A gruesome wave of fatigue swept over her, and she could feel herself folding up like a telescope. Soon she'd be two feet tall. Yet her mind was still functioning, and she seized on her inexplicable fatigue as an excuse. For what man would make a pass at a girl who was totally worn out from working for *him?* She groped for a chair and sat down on it like a dying hippo. "I guess…I guess I pushed myself too hard today." But she could see that he wasn't buying.

He reinforced that impression with sound. "By God, you *are* afraid of me. What do you think I'm going to *do* with you?"

"I'm a little dizzy. I'll be all right. It's just that—" It was such a lousy performance that she knew he'd soon yell "cut" and they'd start the scene all over.

"I see," he said, a touch of impatience in his voice. "You're dizzy."

"Well, I didn't want to tell anyone, but—" Here it comes. Copout No. 436.

"But what?"

"I'm pregnant." It just came right out of her mouth, those infamous two words, supposed to stop men cold in their desire and dead in their tracks.

But he laughed so hard that she figured the windows would surely shatter. He literally staggered backward and had to lean against the desk. "Who's the lucky guy?"

"A boy named Roland. He's with the State Department…" Deeper and deeper.

"Is that so?"

"Oh, yes." She was sinking. He was chuckling, and she was sinking, because a lie is a lie is a lie, and he knew, he knew, he knew.

"You don't *look* pregnant. What month are you in?"

"Fourteenth." She said it because it seemed her only way out. When pregnancy fails, try quippery.

He roared, laughed like a lion. Shook like a grizzly and howled like a coyote. What a good joke he must have heard. Then he came over to her and kissed the top of her head just like dear old Dad. "Lovely. And *you're* lovely. And I love you for being nervous." And his hand slid down and touched one of hers. "Now come on."

She ossified right there on the spot. Actually felt the blood in her veins turn to madrilene. She just couldn't believe that her body could so betray what she had always assumed to be her strongest feature—a caustic tongue. Yet there she was, like something out of a Shirley Temple movie. The big bad stranger was offering her a lollipop and a ride in his car and all she could do was break out in a big scarlet *A* on her forehead.

"Come on, Janice. Dinner." She was afraid to look, figuring perhaps that he was standing there naked and that the dinner he was referring to was him. "Janice," he said, softly and maturely. "I made reservations at Le Moal. That's great French food. Now do you want to come with me or would you rather stay here and...abort?"

She wanted to go with him, really, truly. But she was so weak in the knees that..."I have a dinner date."

"Yes. With me." He was not about to let her slink out of it, realizing that the whole square-off was settling down into some kind of offbeat psychological warfare. "So come on, and stop this nonsense."

"No. Really. I *have* a date." She felt sixes and sevens and twenties and elevens. It was beyond her, but she was barely functioning. He turned her toward him, and she knew that she'd have to come up with someone she had the date with. But who? But, of course. Tom Dietrich.

"Now see here, Janice…"

"Tom Dietrich."

"What?"

"*That's* who."

"Now look…off of all your clever patter this morning, I simply don't figure you to be a virgin…or some *other* legendary animal."

"How dare you?" She said it. Actually said it. Good grief.

He pretended not to have heard. "Nor are you married because I checked your application."

"Swine."

"Nor are you pregnant because I know better. Now here's the deal. We're going to have dinner. Then I'm going to take you home—to where *you* live. And I'm going to *leave* you there because I'm very tired and am not sexually aroused, though I cannot promise that at another time you'll get off so easy. Then I'm going to thank you for a very lovely evening. Then I'm going to go home…alone."

"What will you tell your wife?" God, did she say *that*, too?

"My wife is in Bermuda."

"Then that's where *you* should be." She pulled away, on cue. Because she was playing the ingenue in a Busby Berkeley musical. In another moment the magenta spot would come on and she'd tap dance to the door, do a ukulele solo, and dive into a bowl of puffed rice. And for an encore she'd—

He was behind her. His hands were on her arms and he was talking to the back of her head. And he was turned on and revving. "Listen you—just cut it out because—" He spun her around, land she was kissed. Hard and fast and nice.

She knew who and where she was. She knew who was kissing her and why. She knew how it would go from there and when. But she kissed back, long and sweet and well. The fatigue that had been teasing her simply swept over her and possessed her, and the competition was over, and a Roman voice yelled out to the assembled, "Let the games begin."

A dozen dirty labels passed before her eyes. Foremost among them were slut, easy mark, wanton, nymphomaniac. Next came sex-starved, spinster, harlot, tart, social climber, boss fucker. Next came the couch. The *couch!* She was on it. He was on her. Her blood was off to the races. Her heart was somewhere behind her liver. Her breasts were pliant in his hands. His tongue was knocking on her teeth! "Hell-o, there." His legs were forcing hers open. What the hell was she *doing* there? Her hand found his face, and her fingers closed on all the flesh they could gather. She had the iggy impression that she was pulling a rubber mask from a plastic skull. "Yee-*uff,*" said the dead head in her hand, but she held on, drawing her fingers into a tighter ring, squeezing the collapsing face even harder.

Then the face pulled free, and she saw it, hovering above her, five blue streaks—all pointing to its nose. Then the streaks turned purple...and ran red. She was dumb-struck. And god-awful guilty. She had allowed the contest to happen. It had been implicit in her agreeing to work for him. He had done nothing that could have been interpreted as unexpected. She didn't blame him. She wanted to apologize to him. She was *always* apologizing to men. To Brian, and Paul, and Buzz. To Tom Dietrich (if he'd ever materialize). To Luther. Alway apologizing, apologizing. I'm sorry, I'm sorry, I'm sorry...But she said nothing.

The next morning she was back in the steno pool, floundering with the guppies. And she didn't have to say a word to anyone because somehow they all knew. She never referred to the incident again, in spite of the sly grilling from the rest of the girls. Remaining silent somehow added to her caste. Somehow she had become a woman of mystery, a *femme fatale* of unfathomable depths and untold-of experience. She liked that because, in reality, she was about as unfathomable and deep as a lima bean. She was, of course, back to $75 a week again, but none of the gods on Mount Personnel seemed too upset by her sudden tumble from the heights. Apparently it was not the first time that a typist had failed to measure up to F. D. Douglas' expectations. It occurred to Tiger, as she typed her way into the unfolding day, that the comfy-cozy establishment existence she had so quickly embraced had brought with it its own narrow and traditional perils. However, no matter—it was a world of her own choosing, and she was fast moving up in it. Some of the finest people were raping her.

I gave it time. Figured I had to. Somehow it was all too goddamn symbolic to go up against without a true plan. There she was, holed up in the Y like Helen of Troy. Well, I studied that there Marshal House Y. I studied it from every angle, like a surveyor, like I was preparing an invasion. I suppose I could have dressed in drag and walked right in, but somehow that seemed very gauche. Besides, my stubble's a bit too heavy and I'm against wearing falsies on principle. I knew where Tiger worked, too. I knew the firm, the building, the floor. I was like the cat in Les Misérables—*what was his name? Javert? You know, the guy Charles Laughton played. There wasn't a place Tiger went or a move she made that I didn't know about. It was fantastic.*

It made my day, my life. I was her fucking Boswell, recording her every move. I saw the girls she had lunch with, watched her when she shopped for clothes in Alexanders (even thought of sliding into the check-out counter and accusing her of shoplifting; only I didn't think it would've been such a smash hit of an idea). I knew which subway she rode, the sandwich place she stopped off at every night. And I loved the whole bit. It was my own special pursuit of happiness, as guaranteed by the U.S. Constitution. It got so that if she ever turned around and discovered me, and ran up to me and kissed me, and said she wanted to come back, I'd have been disappointed. I watched her the nights she left late from her goddamn job. I watched her that one night when she left around 6 P.M. so damned tired she couldn't walk straight. But it was okay. It was good for her, gave her a nice taste of the slavey world. Fat was still waiting for his shirts to come back, and it was taking so long that I was beginning to worry if he'd sent any out in the first place or, if instead of taking them around the corner to Won Lee, he hadn't just mailed the damned shirts direct to Hong Kong, where some coolies could run them down to the Yangtze and hit them against rocks. My nights were getting pretty unbearable. Because I never did care to go food shopping, I found myself staying alive on a diet of Lorna Doones and Oreos. No word from the folks in the islands, so fuck 'em. I felt a sudden overpowering need for a dog, so I almost stole one; only he didn't turn out to be exactly my best friend because he nipped me and then, for good measure, pissed on my leg before I could get out of the lousy pet shop. Many people in New York have parakeets for pets, birds and canaries. It's easier to housebreak a bird than a beagle anytime. Also, birds don't bark, and though they give you no protection against burglars, you don't have to walk them. A bird, then, when you get down to it, is really man's best friend. With the possible exception of an eagle which, if you criticize its singing, it could fly away with your nose, so don't. I study hard, very hard. But I'm not getting any better in arithmetic, so there goes the new sled they promised me. It's not Christmas yet, but I find myself getting very much with the Christmas spirit and may shortly steal something big and Yuletidy, like the Salvation Army.

18

The man at the other end of the telephone line was not Luther, as Tiger had first suspected. Nor was he Fred Douglas, who, already back from Bermuda, was already out in Chicago on some kind of Sherman antitrust case. The man on the phone was someone entirely else and entirely new. He identified himself as Steven Larrabee, and went on to say that he was calling at the suggestion of Martha Wesloski, who had previously told Tiger that the man in question was young, personable, eligible, and on the way up. Tiger remarked that he sounded like a smiling young balloonist, but Martha let it go, going on to say that a definite plus in the man's favor was that he did *not* work for the firm. Repeat. He did *not* work for the firm. The prevailing opinion among the girls in the steno pool was that the firm was a way station for just about every overstimulated lawyer in town. Therefore, any man who did *not* work for the firm, regardless of his occupation, be he plumber or philosopher, stood a halfway decent chance of being halfway decent. Also, there was no way in which Steven Larrabee could *ever* work for the firm because he was not a lawyer, or a plumber, or a philosopher—he was an optometrist. Also, and the main reason that Tiger said yes to his offer of dinner, was that she had not had dinner out in a hundred and fifty years, and those hero sandwiches were getting to her, threatening her digestion and haunting her dreams. So, "Yes, Mr. Larrabee. Yes, yes, yes."

The restaurant was semiexpensive and totally Russian. Balalaikas and the Red Army Chorus floated through unseen Muzak vents. The lights were low, the chafing dishes bright copper, and Tiger—for the first time in many a day—relaxed and enjoyed herself. The man across from her, Steven Larrabee, was reasonably attractive and just short of being thirty. As a result of his upbringing and his chronology, he was not yet as sure of himself as he *would* be in a few more years. Therefore, in keeping with her ability to more or less be like the man she was with, Tiger was youthful and comfortable and happily wide-eyed.

Tiger sat at the table in the red leather booth as though she were a giddy out-of-towner. She wasn't putting Steven on. She was simply being what she was at heart yet never had a chance to be, a tourist in New York. She craned her head a hundred and eighty degrees and sopped up all the atmosphere she could. "Oh, it's great. Really. I love it. Thank you for bringing me here. It's so…Slavic. So Tchaikovsky. I'm sure the food is everything you say."

Steven smiled at her from over the large menu. "You never had Russian food before?"

"Nope. Never. And the smells in here—" She inhaled deeply. "Mmmmm. Kiev in the spring."

He laughed. The girl was exactly as advertised. And within five minutes of meeting her he had married her, fathered two sons by her, and built a split level in Connecticut to house the togetherness of their next fifty years. Yet never once did he copulate with her…that's how much he respected her. "What do you *usually* eat?"

"Hero sandwiches. Big ones. Impossible ones."

"Which is your favorite?"

"Turkey, provolone, tongue, chives, water cress, chopped liver, spumoni, Smucker's blueberry jam, garlic, and thousand island dressing on a soft roll."

"When Martha told me to call you she didn't mention that you were out of your mind."

"Actually, *you're* the one who's crazy. Which is why *I* seem crazy. Why, I'll bet, when you talk to yourself in a mirror, it all seems perfectly natural. When *I* talk to myself in a mirror, the words come out backwards, which, if you think about it, is exactly what *should* happen. Besides, what you're doing talking to yourself in a mirror is beyond me. Why do you do that? Check that out." Her eyes dove into the menu. "Ah, the bill of fare. Food fit for a czar."

The waiter appeared, replete with napkin over his arm. He hovered over the pair of diners like the Spirit of the Russian Revolution. He was surly and impatient and spoke with a trace of dialect. "Yes. Your order, please. The kitchen closes soon, and there vill be no axcaptions."

Tiger looked up at the waiter because she knew that voice. She also knew that face. Luther nodded back at her as if to say "good evening." He had an order pad ready and was tapping it impatiently with the stub of a pencil in an effort to hurry Steven along.

Steven, with a winning kind of ingenuousness, was immediately intimidated. He looked at his menu, fully cognizant of the fact that time was running out. He smiled wanly at Tiger. "I'm going to recommend that you have the blinichik. Yes. You'll like that. *Or* you might just prefer the shashlik. Or even the lulu kebab." It dawned on him that he had skipped something. "Or perhaps you'd like to have a drink first? How about some nice red wine?"

Tiger's mouth was so tight that the words could barely squeeze through. "I'll have a cup of hemlock."

"Pardon?"

"Wine would be nice." She smiled.

Relieved, Steven looked up at the stone-faced Rasputin. "Do you have a wine list?"

"No. We are all out." Luther said that with severity and finality, his Rasputin eyes searing into Steven's as if to hypnotize and then drive to suicide.

"Oh," said Steven. "Well...a nice red wine then. And chilled. And a whole bottle, please."

"I'll give you two halves."

"No whole?"

"Two halves."

"Oh. All right. But chilled, okay? Nice and cold."

"One vill be cold. One vill be...eh. Both vill be vite."

"No red?"

"Vite."

"Oh," said Steven, as he struggled to regain command of the situation. "Well, we'll have one blinichik and one shashlik." He smiled across to Tiger. "You can try them both and keep the one you prefer."

Tiger nodded that it would be fine. She wanted to kill

Luther. And she wasn't surprised to see her fingers coiling about a bread knife.

Steven looked up, to reconfirm his order, but Luther was gone. Steven was nonplussed. "Waiters. I swear. Do you think he got our order?"

Tiger shrugged, knowing full well that they hadn't seen the last of the phantom waiter. "He'll be back."

"So," said Steven, suddenly beginning to bug Tiger with his predictability and all-American charm, "tell me about yourself. How long have you been in New York?"

Tiger responded with some inanity, but her eyes were on the action taking place some five yards beyond Steven's shoulder. A little round waiter had come out of the kitchen, balancing a heavily laden tray. He had just set the tray down on a serving table, preparatory to rolling it to the customers who had ordered it, when Luther darted out of the shadows and, in one fluid move, got behind the table and rolled it right up to Tiger and Steve, where he then began to plop the steaming dishes onto the table. And very rudely.

Tiger clenched her eyes shut, and her mouth, too, so as not to see and not to explode. Steven's good nature and trusting character began to take flight. He looked up at Luther. "Say, what are you doing?"

Luther continued to ladle out the sizzling food, plopping and slopping it all about as though he were feeding hogs, much of it missing the plates. "It's all right," Luther said reassuringly. "You vouldn't be sorry. The kitchen is closing quickly. I had to take what I could gat. You'll like this. Soup Siberia, a great delicacy among prisoners. And here, look, Noodles Molotov. You put a match to it and throw it at a tank and—do you have a match?"

"Now wait a goddamn minute…"

Luther dropped the act and stopped the serving. He leaned across the table and clamped a big paw about Tiger's wrist. "Let's go."

Steven stood up. He wasn't as tall as Luther, but he wasn't afraid. "Listen, you—" And he made a fist that seemed less of an optometrist's and more of a coal miner's.

With her free hand, Tiger reached across to grab Steven's arm, to dissuade him, and for a moment they all three looked as though they had joined hands on the top deck of the *Titanic*. It wasn't necessary for Tiger to have interceded. Steven never had a chance to display the tiniest bit of righteous indignation, for two large waiters materialized on the scene, the smaller of them easily as tall, as well as fifty pounds heavier than Luther. The pair of them gathered about Luther and made a large sandwich of him, pressing against him so noticeably that Tiger could have sworn that Luther would shoot up like a squeezed banana. Instead, Luther was spun about quickly, like a toy soldier doing an about-face, then carried off, his feet never touching the floor.

The manager was there, addressing Steven with a sickly angelic smile. "Please. My apologies. This man is not a waiter."

Luther, struggling between the matched set of giant Russian bookends, evidently overheard and shouted back, "Gimmee a chance! I'll be a *great* waiter!" His opinion only hastened his departure.

The manager still felt compelled to explain to Steven. "Sometimes…crazy people. You know."

From farther away Luther cried out. "If not a waiter,

let me be a *singer!*" And somehow he pulled free of his massive captors and, jumping up onto a table at which four people from Schenectady had been dining, he burst into a loud semi-Russian song that could best be described as lousy. "Yol-donka, dov-yuldski—in Moscow, mine luff!" He finished up like Jolson, but with one foot in sour cream. Rude hands reached up at him, and he was pulled offstage like a bad vaudeville act getting the hook…only to reappear nearer toward the door, bobbing up like a Boris-in-the-box. "How about a *juggler,* heh?" His hands found a tureen of borscht, and up into the air it floated, descending onto people like a giant beet shot squarely between the eyes. "And for my naxt number—"

For his next number he hurled more food, mostly borscht. And the patrons screamed because what goes up must come down, and it was coming down on them, a maroon monsoon. Somehow an ignited candelabrum with twelve candles took to the air and, before settling onto a Ukrainian cream pie, triggered the sprinkler system. It added brilliantly to the esthetic chaos.

The waiters, by then numbering five, all of them as large as the Kremlin, no longer chose to be delicate with Luther. They went at him—hard. He took many good cuffs but fought back valiantly, landing a few belts of his own while screaming at them in what he figured was Russian profanity. "Moznik! Fla! Fla! Grib-*donska,* duv yippies! Zush-*nikki,* kak sookers!"

The conflict grew, and more Americans became involved. Men from St. Louis and ladies from Philadelphia, furious at what had become of their quiet repast, began to flail at whoever came close, some of them sensing an opportunity to beat the check, others more pragmatically conjuring up future legal actions. And still others, incensed at Russian duplicity, took pleasure in beating their fists at some of the smaller Russians on the premises. And that included the manager, not of Russian descent at all, but an escaped Hungarian who was gagging on the borscht and was getting pretty sick of the whole act without any help from irate Americans.

Large bowls of borscht, evidently the specialty of the house, took to the air as if launched from Leningrad. At an altitude of eight feet they overturned, and it was "borscht away." The big room soon took on the likeness of a butcher shop in Green Bay. The borscht flowed like blood. Noodles hung onto chandeliers. Babkas exploded like hand grenades. Czar Nicholas and Princess Tatiana and Anastasia were being avenged. Steven stood his ground in borscht-soaked disbelief. It had all happened so quickly that he couldn't quite accept it. Tiger, on the other hand, though furious with Luther's caper, still went wading and swinging into the crowd in an effort to reach him. "Leave him alone! Leave him alone!" She made some headway but never quite reached him, for someone in the crowd was grabbing her ass. She never saw who it was, but it occurred to her, fleetingly, that in every riot—in every revolution—there had to have been ass grabbers. Robespierre and Marat. Patrick Henry, Castro, Lenin and Che—ass grabbers all.

Women were shrieking as only woman could. Someone shouted "Fire!" But there was no fire because borscht, though it simmers, never burns. Luther was being dragged inexorably toward the door, knocking things every which way with his long, windmilly arms, all the while trying to call to Tiger, his voice towering decibels above the crimson bedlam. "Janice-novnik! Janice-novnik, mine luff!"

Then he was hurt, hit full face with a heavy serving spoon, his nose barely missing being broken. But the blood came gushing just the same, pouring from the twin spigots that once were his nostrils. He was a spouting gargoyle and was about to comment on it to a lady nearby when a heavy fist hit him flush in the face again, and his legs wobbled, and he sagged, and he was going down, except that strong arms held him up, anxious to get him to the door, and in his semiconsciousness he emitted an animal sound so terrible that Tiger would never forget it. It was the sound a beast made upon comprehending its own murder in the slaughterhouse pillory. It reverberated throughout the restaurant so horribly that it immediately caused an instant calm. It had been the last wail of a dumb creature, the all-clear, the bell at the end of a bloody bout.

No sooner had Luther been hauled like a lump from the premises and deposited only God knew where than did sanity and tranquillity come out of the paneled walls to reclaim their places in café society. The diners were aided in their return to civilized comportment by waiters who quickly broke out clean linen and wide smiles. Everything grew quiet again. It was as though the incident had never occurred, the battlefield swept clean, the charnel house boarded shut. All those respectable people, dining with extended pinkies—in spite of the fact that the ceiling dripped stalactites of borscht for twenty more minutes. The elegant tinkle of silver and crystal reintroduced itself into the middle-class milieu, and the diners wanted it that way because they didn't care to remember how basely they had behaved in the crisis, how grotesquely they had beaten at the nameless pariah as he was dragged, swollen and beaten, to his offstage fate.

Steven found Tiger standing against a wall, borscht dripping down her seemingly uncomprehending face. "Janice? You all right?" She smiled, but just barely, her eyes still traversing the premises—Howes Caverns seen through rose-colored glasses. Nor was she clearly able to distinguish between real and unreal. Because, for a moment back there, a waiter went crazy. And because of his dreadful affliction, the citizens struck him again and again and then threw him away, resuming their bacchanal as soon as the sacrifice had been consummated. Therefore, the question arises: What century is this? Where are we in time? Is there really a Luther? If so, where does he come from and where does he go? And how can he, at any time of his choosing, come through the window of her life, flash his mad smile, and make her sing like Trilby? "Janice? Hey, Janice?" Steadying hands on her arms. Enter reality. She looked into Steven's face and sent out a smile which she hung on a shrug and then said, "Sorry."

"Janice...what the hell was *that?*"

"That was Luther."

"Who's Luther?"

"Nobody seems to know."

"Come on. I'll take you home."

"Yes. Indianapolis."

"Come on."

• • •

It came as a surprise to me. I mean, the way I couldn't bail out, the way I got all hung up in that Russian waiter bit and couldn't shake clear of it. Usually, I can kick an identity as soon as it's over. But that time—well, it was weird-o-rama. I couldn't shuck it. I was really the guy, really screaming at them in what, I guess, was Russian. (Shades of a former life, eh?) It was like being trapped in a false face that you couldn't get off. Yes, somewhere in another life—yes, I may well have been Kerensky or Trotsky. I'm not too pleased with that because I'd much rather be of royal stock. But I have no recollection of a winter palace or a dacha on the Volga, only of long, cold Siberian winters. Come to think of it, I was probably of Mongol stock with just a touch of Magyar. I mean, the way I rode a horse as a kid—crazy and screaming, pretending to decapitate my governess—I'd have to have been one of Attila's rough riders. The very least that I could have been was a Cossack. The point I'm getting at is that I'm totally convinced that the reason I couldn't shake off that waiter identity was that in assuming such an identity, I had unknowingly scraped a nerve in my memory that wouldn't turn off. Freud called it "ancestral memories." They're recollections old as time. Passed down from when man first started. Passed through the sperm and the egg and the blood and into the cerebellum. And every once in a while, all of us get a glimpse of what we used to be like maybe eons ago. The more I think about it, the more convinced I am that such was the case that night in the restaurant. Borscht must be to me what liquor is to an alcoholic. (Borscht Anonymous?) It just tripped me off, and I was away on a bender. The rotten thing was that those son-of-a-bitching Bolsheviks left me head down in a garbage can. I was drowning in the potato peelings of my origins. I think it took me an hour of flailing to seep out of that fucking quagmire. Also, and this is out-and-out weird, I didn't go right back to my pad. No, I went to the Russian embassy to claim political asylum. (Play that on your Nikita Khrushchev.)

Only I wasn't allowed in. Those lousy Stalinists, at heart they're Mensheviks. And you know about them. Anyway, it's over now, and I'm fine, though my nose is kind of two degrees left of center and my lower lip is so swollen that it looks as if I'm always sticking my tongue out. I passed a woman on the street, I mean with my swollen lip, and she said, "The very idea!" But I'm healing. No sweat. The truly important thing is that, out of it all, has come a greater appreciation of my Russian heritage. And as a result, I've been absolutely sopping up all the Russian reading I can lay my hands on. I'm particularly fascinated with the idea of violent revolution. It appeals to me, very kicky. Also, I've picked up these pamphlets on Marxism and radical dogma. Most of it's bullshit, but it's interesting reading. Also those underground booklets on sabotage and rioting and bomb-making and political agitation—and illustrated yet. If 1936 ever comes around again, I'm going to Spain and fight in the Lincoln Brigade. Shit, Hemingway did it. I don't say this lightly, none of it, because I seem to have a purpose in life now. I just don't happen to know exactly what it is, but it'll come to me. In the meantime, I'm embarrassed to report that I'm wetting my bed again. If you keep it to yourself, I'd appreciate it because it's not the kind of news a guy likes to have get around. The man who was with Tiger—I know nothing about. He picked her up at the Y, and I followed them to the restaurant in a cab that was driven by, I swear, Moe Hegan. (I trust he was the last of them.) I went for a stroll today, in the park, and I conned a kid into giving me a balloon because no one ever buys me a balloon—I have to get one as best I can. Later—a very strange thing. While I was ambling around, I was kicking this empty tin can, like I was playing hockey. And it rolls under a car. And when I bend down to get it, guess what? Who to my wondering eyes do I discover but Tiger. She was under the car, on the opposite side, leaning on her elbows and smiling at me. It was ultrafantastic. I got up and ran around to hug and kiss her—only she's not there. Gone. Incredible. I looked under twenty-three cars for her, but she wasn't there. It was just a glimpse of her, but it was very unsettling because either I imagined her—which would have been very sick because she was so real—or she was there and, after seeing me, ran away, which would have been very sick on her part. Things like that bother me. They immobilize me and cause me to want to do nothing but stay in bed. I'm in bed right now, and it's—let's see—it's past noon. Two of my teeth have been under my pillow for a week—still no presents. Fat comes and goes and is my only contact with the nether world out there. He gets fatter and fatter every day. Perhaps he's my balloon. That's an interesting thought. I think everyone should have a balloon. I think life should be a circus. With admission free. See the brave gypsy boy free the animal from her cage. Ergo.

19

Steven had taken her back to the Y after the Mad Waiter scene. He wanted to see her to her room, but of course, he was not allowed up. Tiger assured him that she was all right. He said he'd call later to check, but she told him that she didn't like to receive telephone calls. He thought he was getting the brush, but she swore that such was not the case. He asked if he could see her again, which was exactly what she figured he'd ask, and she said yes, but would he not call for a week or so. He left, feeling exalted, convinced that a great relationship had begun.

Tiger stood in the warming shower and the threads of borscht went riveleting down the drain. She remained in the shower for so long that her fingers shriveled into ten tiny prunes. And when she emerged from the shower, it was pushing midnight. She had no way of knowing whether Luther was dead or alive or somewhere in between. She was concerned because at the very end of his bit, he did not extricate himself from his assumed identity. To her that sounded a danger signal. No matter what shtik he performed, when it was over, it was over, and he could drop it as though it had never happened. It was exactly what made him so beautiful—that clock in his head, that wild sense of timing, unerring, never-failing. Why, then, did his clock not report to him that the bit was over *before* he took that fearful clobbering? What had gone wrong with his infallible timepiece? Worse—what did it portend? And how hurt was he? And *where* was he? And why hadn't he called? And should *she* call *him?* But he had no phone. She would have to go to his apartment. How could she do that? Damn.

She had a glass of milk. She had no refrigerator in her room, nor was one allowed. But the milk stayed cold on the windowsill at night. She was displeased with herself because the way in which she was reacting was *not* the way in which she'd have *chosen* to react. She wanted Luther to recede calmly into the background of her life. She never felt that he'd do it willingly or easily, but she always felt that she could handle it if he proved obstreperous. Well, he was now proving obstreperous, and she was *not* handling it. At least, she was not handling it as well as she'd *like* to be handling it.

Twelve o'clock became one o'clock, and one o'clock got to be two, and still the pieces refused to fall into a pattern that Tiger could live with. Questions surfaced that she hadn't allowed up in quite some time. Self, parents, goals, expectations. All had once been conclusions. Now they had reverted back to questions. And the questions became fears, and the fears became horrors, and the horrors begot more horrors, and where was Luther? In what street? What jail? What hospital? What morgue? Sleep came eventually, deep and catatonic, and in it she found all the answers, but when she awoke, they had flown. She wanted to be sick to her stomach but couldn't. She wanted to be depressed but failed. She wanted to stay in bed, but she went to work.

She was once again Stella of the Steno Pool, ward of the firm, another of the little orphan girls for whom a home had yet to be found. One foster parent had already sent her back. When, if ever, would she be adopted again? Martha had been adopted. Martha, her only friend, had found a home in the office of a bald legal beagle, and she didn't see her anymore. Except at coffee breaks, where they pledged faithfully to have lunch soon but never did. Tiger wanted Steven to call, but she panicked because she had forgotten first his name, then his face. She wanted to have coffee and Danish, but she threw up instead. She wanted it to be morning sickness, the result of an impregnation by Luther, but it was indigestion. She wanted to go home, to just outside Indianapolis, sure as God made little green apples, but she didn't. But she *would*. Soon. But not until she'd seen Luther again. She'd have to do that—see Luther again. She'd have to manage that somehow, but without being obvious. She was being female again, designing and conspiring, prideful and hurting. How very, very Byzantine.

I got myself invited to a meeting of some revolutionaries. It was in the Village somewhere. This guy I knew, Thaxter, made this speech and people who called themselves brothers all agreed violently. We had wine and pot, and everybody shook hands—and it was over. But through it all, Tiger kept occurring to me. And I came up with a plan that was magnificently meritorious. Like so. It was reasonable to assume that whatever *she was doing, she'd* have *to think of me and the old pad from time to time. The trick, then, was for me to be* in *the pad at the moment when she was* thinking *of me. If I could do that—a contact could be made. All that remained for me to do was to have enough Lorna Doones and Oreos on hand so that I would never have to* leave. *This I attended to via some deft shoplifting at a nearby Grand Union. And I headed home with enough provisions to hole up for a month. Okay, so you have the scene. I'm loaded up with cookies and milk and I'm climbing the stairs to my pad, got it?... Now...As I get to the top of the stairs, I hear the unmistakable sound of a typewriter. And damn it, if it isn't coming from my apartment. I had arrived not a moment too soon because not only Tiger had thought of me, but she was there* waiting *for me. So...I open the door and the typewriting is louder than ever. And I'm convinced that Tiger is actually sitting there, typing away, three thousand times, "Fuck you, Luther."...Only she's not. She's not there. Not at all. And there's no typewriter there either. And the reason is—she's in the shower. It wasn't a typewriter I heard; it was the water running, in the shower...The bathroom door was open, just a little, and I heard her singing the song I winged in the restaurant, the Russian song. So I grabbed my trusty guitar, and sat down on the floor outside the bathroom, and I played and sang the song with her. And then the bathroom door opens all the way, and I could see her sweet smile, aimed at me. And I could see her sleek body, coming nude out of the bathroom. And when she arrived in the room with me, she had the bad manners to turn into Fat Chance...Well, that truly lumbered me. It just wasn't funny. It wasn't her style. It was beneath her to turn me on like that and then turn me off. Fat had this towel of his, with a design on it like a splashy bird, a big sunblast of orange on a field of electric blue, very rococo, very gay. And for the first time I noticed that the son-of-a-bitch-bastard didn't really walk—he minced. Little*

Jap lady steps…I stopped playing and singing immediately, and tried not to watch him get dressed in that hysterical pink jumpsuit of his, but I had to look because it was fascinating, like watching the Liberty Bell squeezing into a condom. Fat waves this chubby, disapproving finger at me, like a merry old soul, and he proceeds to tell me he'd like a hit on whatever it is I'm puffing. He goes on to say that he thinks I've kicked my pail and that the landlord's been looking for me and that all the electricity's been cut off. Then he says that his butterfly shirts are back from the cleaners and that he sees no more reason for tarrying any longer since he's not being utilized. Then he suggests that instead of mooning around for Tiger, I get a new wench because that is obviously my perversion. To all of that I said, "Fuck you." And the Jumbo Jet buzzes the room a few times before coming to a roost in my best chair, and then he produces an emery board and proceeds to file his nails, which looked to me like the spikes you hook onto a chicken's legs when you sign him up for a cockfight. And since cockfighting was not my long suit, I did not accept his unsubtle challenge. Instead, I just picked up my guitar and began playing, casting not an eye in his direction. So he got up in a snit, and he left, and I'm not sure if I ever saw him again…The point I'm making is this: Tiger had come back. But at the last minute she got scared off, or embarrassed, or something. So she turned herself into Fat, which is why Fat seemed so minty all of a sudden. I mean, you just don't stick a very sexy little girl into a body of a man and expect him to go out and knock over a building…Anyway, I felt very good because progress had been made. And so I stayed there and played and sang for I don't remember how long. When it got dark, I went to turn on a light, and Fat was right—they'd turned off my electricity. I didn't like that, not one smidgeon, because I've always been a wee bit afraid of the dark. But gradually I got used to it and soon came to realize that it was another trick of Tiger's. She was in the room with me and didn't want to give me the satisfaction of knowing she was there. Then, around midnight, she went out the window, across the fire escape, down the telephone pole, and slunk back to her goddamn Y. Is that not a grabber?

20

The big morning. It had come. Huzzah. Tiger was adopted. Word had come down from the personnel tower for her to report to the office of one Walter Miller and she was all a-dither. It was $20 a week more, and she'd be out of the lobster pond. She wondered if Walter Miller would be another Fred Douglas—*i.e.,* an octopus with eight knobby knees. But she just couldn't believe that every member of that firm could be all that horny. There had to be at least one man who was there to do what he had gone to law school for. Time alone would tell.

Oh, happiest of days! Walter Miller was not only camped in his late fifties, but was also magnificently gaseous—a true burper, one of the belching best, and nothing was more ardor-dampening than a burst of the burps. In Walter Miller's case, the burps seem to come at two-minute intervals, and if they *didn't,* Walter Miller would thump his chest with his fist and a nice round burp would emerge like the mating call of the bulbous bullfrog. Tiger immediately loved him.

He was a Rolaid's bonanza, a belled cat who could no more sneak up on an unwary mouse than he could burp to the moon. Elysium!

If there was anything imperfect about Walter Miller as a boss, it was his attitude of all-business. For no sooner had she settled in than she found herself taking dictation. Tiger didn't care to confess to the man not only that she had no grasp of shorthand, but that she could barely handle longhand. So she merely faked it as best she could. Because it was her first day at the post, Walter Miller manifested a wondrous patience. He was so patient that Tiger felt a medal should be struck especially for him, with Pitman clusters. They were only three sentences into the memo and already ten minutes had been consumed. At that rate the memo would be old hat well before its completion. It would arrive at its destination like last week's *TV Guide* and would be read like a military bulletin from the Boer War.

But Walter Miller, grim bulldog, hung in there. "So, though I agree with Harrison's position as to the legal precedents involved, I still feel that it would be in our company's best interests if—" He stopped because Tiger had her hand raised like a traffic cop. "Yes?" he burped.

"Too fast."

He was patient and gaseous. It was his daily double. "How far did you get get?"

"Harrison. Is that one r or two?"

"I believe it's two."

"Yes. Good. Just wanted to be sure." She motioned to him that traffic could resume.

Walter Miller was curious, but in a gentle and fatherly way. "How long have you been working for the firm?"

"I don't really know. Two weeks? I get shifted around a lot."

"Why can't you hold a position?"

"If I held the position people around here *want* me to hold, I could be a star."

Walter Miller had no idea who and what she was referring to. Besides, a bubble had lodged in his chest and he thumped at it with his calloused fist.

"Mr. Miller," Tiger said, "instead of this long-winded memo, why don't you just make a phone call?"

"The memo is to ten people."

"It'd still be faster than me taking dictation. Besides, it'd be so much more *personal* if you called."

Outside, in the steno pool, there was some action taking place that Tiger had no idea of. Luther. He was there. Wearing something that vaguely approximated his idea of a suit. It wasn't all that bad, except the blue jacket was plaid and the green pants were checked. And the necktie, canary yellow, looked randy-dandy on the red-and white-striped shirt.

In his hand, Luther had a small memo pad. It had some names scrawled upon it. In his other hand he held a fistful of dollars that he had successfully collected over the last twenty minutes. He leaned informally against the edge of one of the typists' desks and gratefully acknowledged her contribution. "Thank you. And your name? It's for the card. We're enclosing a nice card."

"Nancy Baldwin." She was not thrilled, having parted with the dollar bill with the same enthusiasm she'd have accompanied the giving away of her last kidney.

Luther wrote her name on his pad. "Nan-cy Bald-win. Thank you, Nancy." And he moved on to another of the typists, Gloria, who tried hard to not be seen, except she was an easy two hundred pounds and was camped in a burnt orange sweater that could be seen on a moonless night, in a cellar, at a distance of fifty lunar miles, by a blind man, looking the other way. "Hi," said the charming Luther, leaning against her typewriter so that she had to stop. "I'm Jimmy Hopkins from Civil Disturbances and Misdemeanors. Myrna Wupperman is getting married, and we're collecting for a nice gift."

"So who's Myrna Wupperman?" It was a fair question because Gloria had never heard of Myrna Wupperman.

Luther smiled at her obvious evasion. "Oh, you know Myrna. Myrna with the brown hair? Down to here? Myrna Wupperman." He glared at Gloria and smiled again at her blatant cheapness. "Come on, how often does a girl get married?"

Gloria dug out a guilty dollar she'd been saving for a sundae afternoon. "I wouldn't know. I've been here four years, and it's cost me over a hundred dollars. Come around when *I* get married, will you?"

Luther knew the odds against that celebration's ever taking place, and he cutely pinched one of her clunky arms. "I most certainly will. And your name?"

"Gloria Upham."

He wrote the name on his pad as if he were Santa Claus. "Good. Thank you, Gloria." He started to move on.

But Gloria delayed his departure. "What are we getting her?"

"A combination charcoal broiler and Swedish pancake platter. You know how Myrna likes to cook."

"Oh...*that* Myrna?"

"Yeah." Luther strode away and approached a small dark girl. Anne, possibly Italian. "Hi, I'm Stanley Garibaldi, from Traffic Violations and Torts. Elsa Manicotti is getting married."

"She *is?*"

"Yeah. Fat Elsa. Can you beat that? Anyway—"

Back in the office of Walter Miller—he was on the telephone. Tiger sat by, listening and smiling. "And after checking out the decision in *McNeil versus Lockhardt*, I feel certain you'll agree that the matter bears further discussion before we commit ourselves to a position that may well be legally untenable." He paused, thumped his chest, and burped Swanee River. "And listen, Tony? Tell Mell Westerfeld, will you?...Well, your office is right next to his, so what's the big deal?...And then ask Mel to tell Jerry Flynn and Lee McCall. Very truly yours, Walter Miller." And he hung up before the party at the other end could say another word.

Tiger applauded like a happy nine-year-old. "Good! Oh, good! That was very good!" And she sat back and smiled at him the way his mother used to do. "Now don't you feel a lot better for it?"

Walter Miller thumped his chest. He went to his desk thermos, but it was empty. "I feel another acid attack coming on, *that's* how I feel. Who do I have to call to get my thermos refilled?" He tried to smile, but it didn't quite happen.

Tiger got to her feet and indicated that he had nothing to fear—she'd be back with a full thermos before the next burp. She left the office, the thermos in her grip as if it were the Holy Grail, and she stepped into the corridor—and into Luther.

"Hi, I'm Wally Abernathy, the school nurse. Phil Werber

has just been arrested on a morals charge and we're trying to raise money—either for bail or a nice filthy book."

Tiger was too flabbergasted to present any emotion other than just flabbergastion. "Luther! Oh! Oh, what are you *doing?* Oh...Luther, I *work* here!"

He displayed his fistful of dollars. "I've got close to twenty dollars. I must tell Fat about this place. He'll flip out."

She blinked at all the money. "What did you do—I don't want to hear!" And she walked away, the thermos tucked under her arm like a football. She tossed the words at him, not the thermos. "You return that money—*all* of it!"

Luther followed her down the corridor. "I *need* this money. I'm raising the ransom to get you back from King Farouk. It has to be in a plain paper bag and dropped from a moving Ferrari on Fifty-seventh Street—if I can only remember where." He got in front of her, blocking her way, and he uncorked one of his more irresistible smiles. "How you doing, cutie?"

She faced him squarely. "I'm doing *fine*. God, you're *crazy.*" She blinked at his costume. "What are you *wearing?*"

"This?" He modeled his outfit, with a hint of mint. "Oh—just something I stole from a Bowery mission on the recommendation of my seeing-eye dog. Do you like it?"

She tried to get around him. "Please...Luther?"

He allowed her to pass, then quickly fell in step behind her, talking to her moving back. "Typing nice words? I hope your vocabulary's improved. You don't say 'shit' anymore, do you? I guess with me out of the way you don't get any more anxiety attacks over boot jobs and things? Still taking the pill? Who you been fucking?"

She wheeled at him. "Don't talk to me? Ever! Not

here—not anywhere!"

She started down the corridor again, but he grabbed her wrists and held her there. The thermos dropped on her foot. It didn't hurt, but she was so frustrated she started to cry. He felt that it was the proper time to sum up quickly. "Fat and Leon are gone. The pad is empty. Come back and make me Jello. We'll be alone. I swear, I swear." He picked up the thermos, first kissing her shoe top. "Tiger, I need you. You're everywhere I look. Everywhere. You had no right to come back and then chicken out." He placed the thermos back into her hands. "Handsome little tyke, what's his name?"

Tiger looked into his eyes, trying to figure him, then deciding not to try. "Perhaps, sir, you have me mixed up with someone else." And she walked around him.

"There *is* no one else!" He was following her again. "Only you. You know that." She wasn't answering, just walking. They passed through an area in which other people were standing and chatting. Luther kept talking to her. "I'll call you, okay? We'll work something out that'll be fair to both sides. Or I'll wait for you outside your Y. I'm sure you'll recognize me. I'll be the one with the broken heart."

"You'll be the one with the broken *nose!*" She had stopped and was holding the thermos in a threatening position. And in front of all the people in the corridor, she verbally laid into Luther. "If you make a scene here, if you do, it's the end, okay! The end, final and forever! Do you understand that? *Can* you understand that? Does this message get through to your infant mortality? You are off limits here! You don't belong! I don't know if you belong *anywhere*, okay? So will you please leave me *alone? Okay? Okay?*" She let it end there and watched it all sink into him.

He backed away, smiling sardonically, striving to be arcane. "Okay. Okay. You win, Esposito. The West Side is yours. Me and the Irishman, we'll stay on our side of town. There's enough action for everyone. But one thing, dago—keep Shapiro off my tail, ya hear?" He walked backward, back up the corridor, like a man making a slow and careful getaway, turning his head sideways to address the people he was passing: "Nobody try to follow, ya hear? Nobody make a move. Nobody knows the trouble I seen." He disappeared down the fire stairs, an apparition, a specter.

Among the people who had seen and heard it all was Martha. She came over to Tiger, who was standing motionless, blanched. Martha wanted to know what that had all been about. But it was apparent to her that Tiger either wouldn't talk or couldn't talk. Martha went about her business. Tiger eventually filled the thermos with water and returned it to Walter Miller. Whatever else was in her mind was too muddled for her to attempt to unravel.

It was her denial that hurt me more than anything. It was bad enough that she chewed me out in public like that, in front of all those apprentice moron types—but it was her denying that she had come back to the pad that was the most unstringing. It wasn't like her. I sat in the dark in my apartment until I lit a candle, for, as the saying goes, it is better to light a candle in the dark than to play guitar without being able to see the chords. The longer I sat there singing, the more obvious the truth became. It was awful, unbearable, unacceptable—but it had to be faced. I had been rejected. Re-jec-ted. Whomp. Still, it wasn't exactly a new experience for me. It was just that it hadn't happened to me for quite some time. Rejection and I had long ago become bosom buddies. Rejection had been the crummy short story of my life, and small wonder. I was a most unattractive-type kid, skinny and gooney, with black curls and sad eyes that were forever collecting cinders. In my first twelve years I collected enough cinders to qualify for a fairy godmother (which, come to think of it, I had; my Uncle Gerald, who danced in Broadway shows). I was the runt of every litter, the one they tossed into the river. The one who, if allowed to live, weakened the species. But somewhere along the line I had determined to reject rejection. And the best way to reject rejection was to reject the rejecter before the rejecter rejected the rejectee. That, I think, pretty much sums up why, in recent years, I had become so mean to people. It was a case of fuck or be fucked, and I was getting pretty fucking tired of the latter, which is why I turned to the former. Better to be the fuckor than the fuckee, a reasonable enough philosophy, you will agree. Then—Tiger. With Tiger, well, when she stumbled into the blood clot of my life, it was all different. I mean, she took all the rejection I could dish out, and still she came back for more. Shit, I had rejected her enough times for three dozen frails to blow their brains out. But she kept coming back like a drunken homing pigeon, the game kid. But the wild thing was, each time I rejected her, I felt the pain at least as bad as she did. I felt it so bad that I could cry, and often I did. So, finally—and who could blame her, not me—she finally had enough of the bullshitty punishment I was doling out and, to save herself, she vamoosed, to see if maybe she couldn't do better in life than hooking up with a rich, derelict kid who's always putting her down. Shit, she was entitled. So it is over. The end. I don't know if she knows it yet (probably), but I know it. I'm not sure if there's anyone new in her life as yet (probably not), but there should be someday. Then again, who knows? But that isn't the issue. The issue is that Tiger and I are not an item anymore. And the reason is that we probably never *had anything going for us in the first place, nothing at all. When we met, she had been reaching out, trying to get out of her world—and I was reaching out, trying to get into it. Hell, I'd like to belong somewhere someday. I don't much care going from day to day with nothing happening except my own slow dying. So there we were— moving in different directions, and happening to meet while we were in motion. And in the process, we waved to each other because it was such great sport. And somehow our hands touched, and lo, if she wasn't everything I wanted, and I everything she wanted. And so it is written that the touch became an embrace and that the two became one. Yet all we did, when you cut through all. that crap, was just stop each other cold and hurt each other hard. It's like a fullback busting through and a linebacker coming up to whack him. Zap. No gain. No loss, but no gain. Anyhow, now that I've got it pegged, I can accept the fact that she belongs in her own comfy world, where she'll take tea and marry some pipe-puffing charming commuter and have blond kids with straight hair, and get broad in the beam, and grow old as graceful as a fucking swan, and die quietly on some nice autumn day when she's a hundred and five all propped up and smiling for her 643 descendants. Whereas I, in my exotic looniness, I will remain on my side of the cage, making funny faces at gum-chewing gawkers, until that one day, in the winter, when everybody stops laughing at my antics and my keeper comes and leads me out into a quarry somewhere and bashes my head in with a Friar Tuck stave and then makes glue out of me. And maybe, once I'm glue, she'll buy me in a bottle and use me to paste her kids' pictures on the walls because, in that way, I'll be able to stick around. Anyway, anyhow, and no matter—the candle is going out, and it gives me the willies. I'll sit here until it's light. In the dark I kind of pretend and make believe that she's still here. Here, kitty, kitty. Here puss, puss.*

21

Tiger spent the remainder of that day typing up some reports for Walter Miller as well as refilling his thermos two more times. And it occurred to her that, just perhaps, it was all that water that was making him burp. Especially since he never went to the john to relieve himself. Perhaps it was his heart saying "Help." Or perhaps his heart, to save itself, was floating around in his lungs somewhere, like a life buoy, burping on and off as a warning to floating cartileges... She tried hard to not think of Luther. But the laugh was a different kind of laugh even to her own ear. It was a laugh, not from the core, but from the perimeter. It was a laugh, not of a participant, but of an observer. Somehow—*click*— she was on the outside looking in. There was Luther, on the stage, dead center as usual, but doing a single. She was somehow in the audience. But she kept changing her seat, moving farther and farther to the rear, until, she was at the box office, getting her money back. Then she left the theater. It had been a fine show, really, with some nice memorable performances. But very little of it stayed with you once you headed home. Oh, there was this *one* actor—very endearing, very good and with his own high style, but he had been dreadfully miscast as the love interest, and he was powerless in a plot that never quite took form. It had been, at best, a pleasant diversion, but it just couldn't sustain. Besides, who could believe it?

She walked back to the Y after work, and it took a few hours because of the concentrated window-shopping she did along the way. The city was quietly pretty that time of day, turning that soft gray-purple that comes just in advance of evening. She felt wistful and decidedly mature. And for the first time in too long to even guess at, she felt peaceful. It would have been a fine time for Christmas. She felt very much like Christmas. She wanted to buy something for someone, but she had no one to do it for. She barely knew Martha. Luther—oh, swell. Still, it wasn't such a bad idea. With her new outlook, Luther no longer seemed an obstacle. Rather, he was slowly transforming into a very fine memory, one she'd warm herself by as the years ticked off. Such being the case, what *could* she get for him? The first thing that occurred to her was a shrunken head; it seemed somehow appropriate. Then she became maternally practical. Gloves, for the oncoming winter. A muffler, a huge one, one that reached all the way to his ankles. One he could wrap ten times around his neck and let the tails fall where they may. And he'd look like a Christmas caroler out of Dickens, and, oh, what songs he'd sing. "God fuck ye, merry gentlemen, let nothing you dismay." She laughed to herself, and it was fine. She could think of Luther with affection. That was fine, too. She had lived, for a while, in that small space between the absence of summer and the oncoming of winter. An eternal fall. She had made her home there, in a tiny time between harvest and Christmas. And she had compressed three decades of love and kisses into one magnificent pendulum ride from amusement to loss. And now it had a period to it. A gentle, soft period, set down in a graceful script by the all-seeing Almighty. No more hurt. No more uncertainty because…no more story. She had made of Luther an old photograph, already turned at the corners, already yellowing and wallowing in the past. She would be twenty soon. A landmark. Thirty was dirty because twenty was plenty. Forty was naughty, but twenty was plenty. The last few blocks to the Y she took with long strides.

At the desk in the lobby of the Y were two phone messages for her. Both from Steven Larrabee. He'd call again later. Steven Larrabee—so *that* was his name. In the elevator she tried it on: Mrs. Steven Larrabee. Larrabee-McAllister nuptials announced. Janice Larrabee of the PTA, wife of a—whatever did he do for a living? She had forgotten.

She inserted the key into the lock and experienced a sudden shudder because the door was unlocked. She nudged it with her foot, as they did in all those movies, and the door fanned open, all the way, in a practiced arc, even creaking just to sweeten the drama. She waited, just a beat, making certain that no one was standing there; then she peeked in. A light was on, dimly. And there, standing before the crucifix that hung on the far wall, facing her with his hands clasped over his belly like a saintly harbinger of peace—yes—Luther. Luther, Luther, Luther. The Ghost of Christmas Present.

Tiger was five steps beyond anger and five others short of comprehension. She solidified where she stood. Abject shock was her bag. A pious Luther was standing before her, like a priest calling at the home of an unfortunate parishioner. His collar was turned around, and he was a curly-topped Pat O'Brien about to talk the men out of a prison riot. What a soul-searing sight. Luther before the cross, God's emissary. "Hi," he said. *"Pax vobiscum* and all that shit." The anger and power of J. Christ were certainly being put to the test.

"Oh, Luther," she said softly, with somebody else's voice, probably that of a grade school teacher. "How did you get in *here?"*

"I told them I was God. They had to let me in because God is so well thought of around here."

She closed the door and stepped into the room. "Luther, I don't *believe* you—the things you *do*. You could be *arrested."*

"Not if I'm God." He genuflected like a spastic atheist.

She studied him and damned if he didn't look like a holy man. And all she could say were her usual famous words: "Oh, Luther."

He picked up the little ballet dancer doll. "I believe, as a parent, I have certain visiting privileges."

She was pleased that he wasn't ranting as he had been doing that afternoon. "Well...you can't keep following me around. You have to stop *someday."*

"Why?" He set the doll down and smiled at her, most benign.

Tiger took her time, gathering her thoughts and constructing her prose so that, perhaps, tonight, it could all be ended, amicably and forever. "I've been thinking about it all day. It was very funny what you did in the office, very funny. And I laughed a lot about it, I really did, but I just don't think life can be laughed at all the time. People...have to be able to accept responsibilities." She had to laugh at her pedagogy. "Oh, listen to *her.*"

He seemed to understand her point, but still spoke calmly in his own behalf. "I collected a lot of money in your office. I could work that whole building and become very prosperous and responsible in a week."

"Luther"—it was becoming increasingly more difficult for her because, as was always the case, he had fixed on a stand and was proving to be immovable—"I think that when I left you, I figured I'd end up going back to you. I did. Really. And that thought...sustained me. It sustained me because, well, because working my way back into the Establishment hasn't exactly been a whole barrel of monkeys. But it doesn't make much sense now. Going back, I mean. You know?"

"Why?"

"Well—what would I be going back to? All you offer me is...limbo."

"It's a very nice place, limbo."

"Oh, sure. A lot of old movie houses. And all we do is go from one to another until all the film runs out. And then what?"

"I don't know. What's playing next week?"

She attacked head on, but with a tender maturity she was pleased to discover in herself. "You know I can't live with you anymore, don't you? You know it as well as I do?"

"All the lights are out in my apartment."

"You didn't pay the electric bill." She was swiftly growing years and years older. He was moving in the opposite direction. "Luther, it was right on the table."

"Everything in the refrigerator died. The Jello died. Three apples died. Four pieces of salami are dying."

Her ship was nosing down in a sea of desperation. Already one man was overboard. "Luther, bills have to be paid. They don't go away. They're part of reality, and reality has to be faced. Well, doesn't it? Don't *we* have to face reality?"

"Yes."

"Well, that's what I'm trying to do. I mean"—her arm shot out like a tour guide's—"look at this room. The height of Presbyterianism, no?"

"Yes. Stay here and you'll always vote Republican. How can you do that when there are still some Kennedys left?"

"But, Luther, this is *me*. This room, it's what I *am*. It's what I come from and—" She smiled at the hurt little boy. "I don't believe I can go on playing Florence Nightingale to your King Kong."

He smiled. "I know."

"Do you? Do you, *really*?"

"Yes."

"Then why did you come here?"

"I picked up your scent. This building is upwind of my pad."

"No. You came here to talk me into coming back to you."

"No."

"Yes. I *know* you Luther."

"No, you don't." And maybe she didn't. He was so passive, so quietly convinced of what he was saying. "I came here to tell you good-bye. We never said it. It got lost in the shuffle."

She felt her equilibrium failing. If he was plotting something, she didn't want to fall into the pit of it. "Luther, we're playing word games. I can't do that anymore. I can't. And I'm not going to let you trap me. I'm not going to say 'I love you' because it implies commitment, and I can't commit to you, because *you* can't commit to *anything.*"

"I know."

She was Japan fighting China. She had superior arms, but how could she win when all he did was drop back and encircle? She would have to make one strong offensive thrust at the heart of things, so she stuck her hand out toward him. "Luther, good-bye and—well, good-bye."

He stood his ground, just smiling and nodding his head in agreement. If she wasn't careful, he'd agree her to death.

"Luther, I'll…see you around." Her hand was still stuck out in the air, stiff, certain, unwavering.

He didn't take it. He just kept smiling and nodding, as if knowing that once he clasped that hand, it would be the end of it, so long and farewell.

"Maybe Disneyland." She smiled. "I'll see you in Disneyland, okay?"

"It's a big place."

"I'll find you."

"Well, I'll be the third ride from the left as you come in."

"Okay."

"If you can't find me, ask a guide."

"All right."

"They're very good. They have to deal with a *lot* of lost kids."

"I know." She looked at her hand, that dumb appendage, still sticking in the air. It was like a gun pointed at his heart. And it had a hair trigger, so look out.

"Well…"

"Good-bye, Luther."

"Right." He reached out and took her hand and pumped it as though he had just met up with an old football buddy. "Right."

"Right." And she prepared to remove her hand from his, convinced that when she tried to pull it free, it would stay glued there, forever, which, Lord knows, if she had the bad judgment to follow her idiot heart, was what she wanted. But the hand came easily free, and she was naked and friendless, and would surely die if he didn't grab her, and wrap her up, and take her home, and figure out a way to pay for her later.

But all he did was nod and walk slowly to the door. And if it took him much longer to get there—Go, Luther, go. Stay. Go. Die. Shit.

His hand was already on the doorknob when he turned and came quickly back to her, to hug her, she hoped, and tell her she was nuts and that it was *not* over because it could *never* be over. Instead, he thrust something into her hand and started out again, saying as he was leaving. "You're the only person in the world I'd ever give that to. It's worth fifty dollars."

She looked at the little pink card in her hand, a Monopoly card. A Take-a-Chance card. "Get out of Jail Free." She looked up, about to laugh, and he was already gone. The door was still closing. The door closed. It set in cement and grew covered with dust and mold. And grass sprung up around it. And Ivy impeded its ever being found again. And already the mourners were gathering, and all of them were her. Farewell, Luther. Godspeed. Send me Christmas cards. And if you ever find your way, won't that be somethin' grand?

22

The next day in the office Tiger knew that she had turned a big corner. Whatever she was to be, all of it lay ahead. Much of it would be trial and error, some of it pithy and dull, lots of it annoying and painful, but bits of it—small tinies of it—would be fruitful and worthwhile. It would be like panning for gold. It would take time and torture. There'd be false hopes and terrible disappointments. But one day she'd come upon it, and it would be the biggest thing since the Comstock Lode.

She typed away at Walter Miller's reports, working loosely and well. No mistakes, no deliberative pauses. Just on and on, Tessie the Typist, a working girl out of Dreiser. Who will buy my violets? And who will be my love?

The door to her small private office opened, and Martha shone in. "Hey? Where's your boss?"

Tiger looked up from *Wagner v. North Dakota*. "He went down to the drugstore for a Bromo or something. Why? What's up?"

Martha was not concerned. "Oh, we have to evacuate the building."

"What?"

"Yeah. Another of those crazy bomb scares."

"No kidding? Okay." She got up.

"A phone call to our switchboard. Called himself the Mad Bomber of London. Awful lot of lunatics running around this city. Anyway, shake it up. I'll meet you downstairs. We'll have lunch." Martha disappeared.

Tiger stood there and sighed and smiled. And she thought, Oh, Luther. And she looked down at her desk so piled with work, so much to do. And even as she heard the people scuffling through the halls, she figured she'd better sit down and attend to the typing.

Outside, the building was emptying, the revolving door scooping up people as they came out of the elevators, then paddling them out into the street. To most of the evacuees it came as a welcome respite from the day's drudgery.

On the ninth floor Tiger went clackety-clack and the words danced off the ribbon and onto the paper. Clackety-clack, party of the first part, plaintiff against the state, whereas and heretofore, and in lieu of and notwithstanding. Then she stopped. Abruptly. Her fingers froze on the air. And the horror of it spun ten times around in her brain and then came screaming through her eyes. For it had all taken frightening shape...And she knew. Mommy, Daddy, Mommy, Daddy...

It was a loud noise, enormous and ricocheting. A flash of shock white. Then a roar. Then a crumbling of superstructure and an agonizing twisting of girders, and a cloud of collapsing plaster giving birth to flying photographs and ripped swatches of wall. Carpet curled and tiles popped up from lavatory floors. And glass continued to shatter long after…tinkling bells, sleighs going o'er the fields to Grandma's. And somewhere within the monstrousness of it all, a young girl, who had just been passing through this world, saw her skirt come flying above her head and then saw nothing more.

Did I ever tell you about the time I walked backwards all the way to Newark? That was no mean trick. It took three months to accomplish, and the bore of it was that it received no acclaim. Shit, people go over falls in barrels and waltz through fire nude, stupid things—dumb— and they get public reverence. But walk backwards to Newark, through traffic and rain, and you might just as well have stayed in Passaic for all the recognition you gain. It was then I knew that whatever I was to make of my life, it would all be done without anyone caring. The first hint I ever had of the "alone road" I was to go had nothing to do with Newark. It had to do with that terrific nosebleed I had in the middle of the night when I set the alarm for 11:45 P.M. because it was New Year's Eve and I wanted to get up and smack together two dishpans I had stuck under my bed for just that purpose. I smacked them together, all right, but I got my fucking nose caught between them and nobody heard my screams because they were all having such a good time with Guy Lombardo, bringing in 1947. So I bled like a stuck pig while the world cheered. It may interest you to know that I almost died.

• • •

On Madison Avenue there was chaos and disbelief. The large office building still stood, but up there, the whole ninth floor was sticking out like a xylophone of busted dinosaur ribs. Charred beams protruded, hanging over the street like tank barriers. And loose wires, exposed ganglia, fluttered and groped about in search of new veins to solder onto. Smoke and dust billowed out, and a light ash filtered down like a volcanic snow, ever so delicately, and ever so sad.

Snow is interesting because it never falls the same way twice. Nor does it make any noise. If snow could speak, I guess it would say "look out." Snow, I had been told early on, was Angel Dandruff, a rather unpleasant thought if you think of all the nice people supposedly up there, floating around and singing religious ditties and fucking on the wing, and all of them with dandruff. Yacccch. If snow is Angel Dandruff, then does it not follow that rain is God's sweat? And if you think about it, isn't that right and proper? Because shouldn't that cunning old son of a bitch do a little sweating over the miserable job he's doing? And if you stay with that line of thinking, can't you pretty much get a picture of what the old fraud is doing up there when we get floods and mud slides down here? *Isn't it all a part of the chronic dysentery that the ever-loving Lord has been contending with since He first gave earth life through his majestic seven-day defecation? The cure for all mankind, then, is huge doses of Ex-Lax, shot into the sky in place of rockets. And like that one particle of sperm that survives the acid of the vaginal tract, maybe one little chunk of Ex-Lax will find its way up the Almighty's ass and then, maybe, we can get a little peace and quiet down here. Let us pray.*

. . .

At street level the fire engines were at work, ladders groping skyward, snaky hoses dowsing everything within their reach. Emergency vehicles were on the scene, huffing and sighing. And firemen in helmets and slickers, looking like unsheathed penes, ran this way and that, shouting to one another like players in a losing game. The police were already fencing off the crowd, and the injured were at work probing dirty fingers through each other's superficial wounds. Ambulances gathered in fitful bunches, and white-jacketed interns scattered out like escaping convicts. Debris littered the street, cars covered with chunks of cement and slivers of glass. Sirens wailed in the manner of keening widows, while underneath the street, subways continued to mole in oblivious patterns to Queens and Brooklyn and the Bronx.

Many of the building's former occupants stood about counting noses. Martha was there, scanning the crowd, searching for Tiger, whom she had not seen come out of the building. Walter Miller, burping like a grease gun, came by, and Martha grabbed his arm and, disdainful of rank, asked him if he'd seen Janice McAllister anywhere. He hadn't.

Some fifty yards away from the heart of the action and well beyond the police barricade, the tall young man stood, leaning dispassionately against a mailbox.

I don't see her, do you? I don't know what she was wearing. I guess it was something on the order of a pert blouse and a neat skirt. She's about twenty years old with brown eyes and kind of dirty blond hair, natural, so it tends to be kind of tawny. She answers to the name Janice, but some of you may remember her by her heathen name, Tiger. If you see her, please report it to the lifeguards. She's forever wandering off. Her parents are terribly worried, and I myself have come from a very busy day to look for her. Anyway, keep your eyes open, or you're liable to miss her. And nobody wants that.

Walter Miller and Martha Wesloski and some others were in their panic. They grabbed out at policemen in motion. They voiced their fearful suspicion to firemen. Perhaps Janice McAllister was still up there. If she was, she'd be dead, said the only fireman they could get a reaction from. But perhaps she'd gotten out. Officer? Officer!

Pretty day. And the ocean's so calm you could stick a canoe on it. And I hate to bother you with my problem, but this girl, she wandered away from the umbrella at about, oh, I'd say two o'clock and—shit, oh dear—there she is. Thank God. Hey! Tiger? Yoo-hoo! Over here! Here I am! I'm waving, you dummy, can't you see me? Right! Attagirl! Come on!…Well, that's a goddamned relief. I was really worried. But, as you can see, she hasn't a mark on her from that nasty wave that tumbled her over. I suppose I should act immediately angry and scold her. You're supposed to do that when a kid walks away, you know. But if you don't mind, I'll dispense with that kind of horseshit. I am so damned relieved, I—Here, Tiger, Here, puss puss. Come on, baby…Hi.

• • • •

Hi.

> *Okay.*
> *Take my hand.*
> *Gotcha.*
> *Spoons up?*
> *Spoons up.*

Great wits are sure to madness near allied,
And thin partitions do their bounds divide.

—JOHN DRYDEN

SUMMER OF '42

Captivating and evocative, Herman Raucher's semi-autobiographical tale has been made into a record-breaking Academy Award nominated hit movie, adapted for the stage, and enchanted readers for generations.

In the summer of 1942, Hermie is fifteen. He is wildly obsessed with sex, and passionately in love with an "older woman" of twenty-two, whose husband is overseas and at war. Ambling through Nantucket Island with his friends, Hermie's indelible narration chronicles his frantic efforts to become a man, especially one worthy of the lovely Dorothy, as well as his glorious and heartbreaking initiation into sex.

MAYNARD'S HOUSE

Austin Fletcher, a disturbed young Vietnam War vet, is willed a small house deep in the woods of northern Maine. He comes to own it by the generosity of a brother-in-arms—a fellow soldier and confidante, Maynard Whittier, killed in action by a wayward mortar shell. The rugged landscape of Maine is an intoxicating blend of claustrophobic interiors and endless frozen wastelands. Little by little, the mysterious force in the house asserts itself until Austin isn't exactly sure what is in his mind and what is real. And just when our hero's had enough and is ready to quit the place, a blizzard arrives and the real haunting begins.

THERE SHOULD HAVE BEEN CASTLES

Ben is the writer who can't seem to make it; Ginnie is the dancer who can't seem to miss. In 1951 they are two scared kids in love–determined to hold onto each other no matter what. Together the world is theirs for the asking.

In the exhilarating landscape of 1950's show biz, from the neon glamour of the New York stage to the starry glitter of Hollywood, they have love and success—pure, intense, and perfect. It should go on forever, fueled by enough romance and glamour for all the record books and fairytales that ever were. But can their love prevail or will it all come tumbling down due to an unexpected twist neither of them could have foreseen?

Printed in the USA
CPSIA information can be obtained
at www.ICGtesting.com
JSHW031841260624
65440JS00019B/707

9 781626 818927